HOW FAR WE GO AND HOW FAST

NORA DECTER

ORCA BOOK PUBLISHERS

Library and Archives Canada Cataloguing in Publication

Decter, Nora, 1986–, author
How far we go and how fast / Nora Decter.

Issued in print and electronic formats.
ISBN 978-1-4598-1688-6 (softcover).—ISBN 978-1-4598-1689-3 (PDF).—
ISBN 978-1-4598-1690-9 (EPUB)

I. Title.
PS8607.E423H69 2018   C813'.6   C2017-907554-3
C2017-907555-1

First published in the United States, 2018
Library of Congress Control Number: 2018933723

Summary: In this novel for teens, Jolene copes with her brother's disappearance
by playing his guitars and shutting herself away from the world.

*Orca Book Publishers is dedicated to preserving the environment and has
printed this book on Forest Stewardship Council® certified paper.*

Orca Book Publishers gratefully acknowledges the support for its publishing
programs provided by the following agencies: the Government of Canada through
the Canada Book Fund and the Canada Council for the Arts, and the Province of British
Columbia through the BC Arts Council and the Book Publishing Tax Credit.

Edited by Sarah N. Harvey
Cover design by Meags Fitzgerald and Teresa Bubela
Cover image by Meags Fitzgerald
Author photo by Nicholas Lefebvre

ORCA BOOK PUBLISHERS
orcabook.com

Printed and bound in Canada.

21 20 19 18 • 4 3 2 1

HOW FAR
WE GO
AND HOW
FAST

To my dad, who first told me about time.

PROLOGUE

This is a travel story. About a trip I take in my head.

When I need to get away, I go back to 2001. I was eleven, and my brother, Matt, was sixteen, the age I am now, except when he was my age he knew everything. He knew normal things, like how to drive and how to make conversation with his peers. But he also had specialized knowledge, like how to get onto the roof of the parking garage downtown where you could see for days in any direction, how to avoid getting jumped waiting at the bus stop or walking down the back lane and how to handle Maggie, our mom. He knew everyone on the block and everyone knew me, because I was his sister.

We were in the middle of a cold snap when Matt got the call that his guitar was ready. The kind of cold snap that comes so late in winter, everyone tries to deny it's happening because spring is so long past due. Times like that, prairie people refuse to put their good boots back on—they leave the extra layer of wool at home and then suffer for it. Matt hung up the phone and reached for his coat.

I know now but I didn't know then that a guitar maker is called a luthier. Our luthier was named Sven, and his workshop was an hour north of the city, in Gimli, an Icelandic town on the shores of Lake Winnipeg. Matt had been up there a few times over the course of that winter to consult on the type of wood the guitar would be made of, the shape it would take. He came back buzzing from these meetings, all lit up. I imagined they were building something holy, saw Matt's drives to the workshop as pilgrimages.

Maggie was out with the car the day Sven called, but it didn't matter, Matt said there was a bus from the station downtown that went out there. In the name of nothing better to do, I went too. We listened to his Walkman on the bus, one headphone each, the cord jerking out of my ear because Matt couldn't keep still.

Having a guitar built is an insane extravagance for a teenage boy. But Matt never spent—he just saved and saved. All the money he earned working at the pizza joint over by the casino, where he spent nights sprinkling low-grade shredded mozzarella over dough painted with tomato-sauce brushstrokes, it all went to the guitar.

Sven's place was a few minutes' walk from where the bus dropped us. Matt led me around back to the workshop, which was taller than the main house and nearly as large.

Snow had been falling all day but slowly, with persistence. It traveled unrestricted across the fields beyond the yard.

We had to lift our knees high to clear the drifts. Sven ushered us into the space, which smelled of sawdust and metal. Shelves climbed the walls like bunk beds, guitars in various stages of completion resting in the shadows.

Matt had three guitars already. The first was a little acoustic our dad, Jim, gave him for Christmas when he was nine and I was four, old enough that I remember him without a guitar in his arms, but barely. Then there was Shredder, a red electric that some guy named Bud left behind after a party. To Maggie's credit, when Bud came looking for it a few days later she was like, *Guitar? What guitar?* And then she got him drunk. Meanwhile, Matt was in the basement with Shredder, getting to know new kinds of noise. When he was fourteen Maggie had some kind of windfall and came home with the Gibson. I was nine and just a little jealous of the hours he spent playing guitar. Music was always his thing. I listened, loved every new song he wrote, but by then I was starting to want to be a part of it.

They were all good instruments, he had explained on the bus ride out to Sven's, but the new guitar would be his blues guitar, the one he'd take when he went downtown to jam with the old men at the Windsor.

When Sven handed Matt his new guitar, he reached for it like a father reaches for his newborn child. Even in my ignorance I could see it was a beautiful thing. Warmth emanated from the surface of the wood, like fire from behind a fogged-up window. Dark lines of grain flowed down it like a fingerprint. For a few minutes Matt could not be moved.

He tuned the strings and struck a first careful chord, then another and another. Sven told me quietly that the rosewood had been chosen for how well it spoke. I thought he meant he could hear voices in the wood. I only realized later that there are ways of testing wood for resonance, of measuring the different qualities of sound.

Matt played until Sven's wife appeared at the door in a housecoat and a wool hat to say dinner was ready and would we like to stay. Matt said no, thank you, we had to get home, but he didn't stop playing. Sven patted him on the back and told us to turn the lights off on our way out.

"We should probably go," I said eventually. He looked up, startled, even more so when he saw the clock. Before we left, Matt took off his sweater and tucked it carefully into the guitar case he had brought. I wound my scarf around the long elegance of the fretboard. We ran along the road in ruts left behind by a truck, our heads down, laughing. At the station I stood by the doors with the guitar while Matt went to get tickets. He returned pale beneath his wind-burned cheeks.

We'd missed the last bus. There was another going to the city that night, but it only made a flag stop on the highway. The station attendant said he'd radio the driver and tell him to look for us. Then he said we'd better hurry.

Our cold is dry. It sears your skin, so that you don't feel the pain you're in until you begin to shake with it, a shaking that takes you over, that's more than a shiver—it's a shudder.

At first we sang as we waited at the side of the road in the whistling dark. This song Jim liked to blast in winter.

Matt and I would sing it when we took the dog out on short walks that felt like death marches.

"Let's go to fucking Hawaii," Matt sang.

I jumped in. "Go get drunk in the sun."

But the song died on our lips after the first verse.

"I've also heard fucking Cuba is nice this time of year," Matt said, his shoulders up around his ears. The words barely escaped his clenched jaw before the wind whisked them away. He only had a T-shirt on under his jacket, and he'd begun to shake so fiercely you could have mistaken it for a seizure if you didn't know better.

"Fucking Cuba sounds good," I said.

Soon there was nothing to say that wasn't a comment on the cold. On the prairie you're raised to respect the winter. You're told stories of children who die of snowball hits to the head. Of teenagers who lose fingertips to the frost and of drunks who lie down to rest on a snowbank and never sober up again. As we stood in silence at the side of the road I became aware of how cocky we'd been. We weren't dressed for such an expedition. Matt wrapped his arms around the guitar and pulled his hood down low.

Ten minutes passed. Or was it half an hour? Darkness obliterated the highway. The wind blew, and snow fell sideways. I couldn't feel my toes. Orbs of light appeared and approached like angels, but none of those angels was our bus.

And then a pair of headlights emerged from the black, brighter than the rest, so bright it took a moment to register it really was a bus shuddering to a halt fifty feet down the road.

We ran for it on clumsy, leaden legs, climbing the steps into warmth that set my flesh on fire.

"Is it okay?" I asked as Matt popped open the case to check on the guitar.

"I think so. Are you all right?"

"I'm fine." Snow melted down my face like a sudden onslaught of tears. He rested the guitar case on an empty seat, and we rubbed our hands together to get the feeling back. The bus drove on through the weather, and from the seat in front of us came the terrible, tuneless twang of guitar strings snapping, one by one.

⌒

We got home giddy, our cheeks chapped with wind, but we burned with something else too. The feeling we'd survived something. That we'd been brave.

Maggie was still out, so we took over the kitchen. Matt laid the blues guitar down on the table and began to tend to it, his hands stiff from the cold. I filled a pot with milk, spooned in hot-chocolate powder and stood at the stove stirring, so it wouldn't get that skin on top. When it was ready, I sat on the counter, legs swinging, watching Matt work. He checked the guitar for damage and then began to put on new strings, patiently threading each one through its peg hole, pulling it taut and then tightening it. Finally he tuned up, tilting his head as he plucked the strings and listening as if for an answer. When each one rang true he smiled, then remembered the hot chocolate and took a long drink. "See?" he said. "No harm done."

He strummed, gently at first and then harder, and as the rhythm unfurled into a song, I sang along. I usually only ever sang when we were walking, when we were goofing around, and that was more like hollering anyway. I didn't know how it sounded now or if he wanted me to shut up, but when the song concluded Matt looked up and said, "That sounded good. Let's do it again."

So we played it again, and I wasn't outside the music anymore, I was in it.

When I need to get away, that night five years ago is where I go. I go back to it. I turn around. Go back to it again.

ONE

In the morning there are bodies on the floor. Facedown, three of them, which isn't half bad. One among the shoes kicked off at the door. One cozy in the slot between couch and coffee table. And one half on the floor, half on the loveseat that we carried home fifteen blocks three years ago.

That's Cory at the bottom of the stairs, using a boot for a pillow. He's some kind of cousin of Maggie's, and I don't worry about waking him—he won't wake easily. And that's Roxie, Cory's on-again, off-again, wedged behind the table. I recognize her hair extensions. Loveseat lady must be new, or at least I don't know her from this angle. Howl is waiting in the kitchen. Her tail thumps the linoleum when I walk in, but otherwise she's quiet. She knows the routine as well as I do. We've been running it for a while. She won't get her walk until I've made the rounds, made sure everyone has a pulse. Until then she watches, because she's a watchdog. She sees everything we do and everything we don't do. She sees me chuck a filter in the coffee maker and fill it with a few shakes of the hazelnut shit Maggie keeps around. (The coffee is a concession to the drunks. I don't hate them. I just want them to go.) She sees me crack the window an inch and let in the cold. (To help wake them, clear the air. It reeks in here. Good thing I hold my breath so well.) And she sees me go into the hall to suit up for outside, which must be done with care, so that outside doesn't kill me. All Howl needs is a leash, but I'm a mere mortal, so on go the sweaters, the hat and the scarves. My snow pants are not cool. I wear them anyway. Maggie makes fun, but then, I don't put much stock in Maggie's opinions. She wears high heels to wade into two feet of snow.

One more thing before we go. Smoke raid. Creep around the living room, shaking packs. The table packs are empty, the jacket-pocket packs have too few to spare, but on the floor beside loveseat lady I hit the jackpot. Pack of du Maurier, three-quarters full. I take five. Risky, but there are empty bottles everywhere, and that's just what they drank after closing down the bar. No one's gonna have a solid count on how many smokes they should be waking up to.

Stealing is stealing, says Howl from the doorway. *Doesn't matter if they notice or not.*

Not true, I say. *There are different degrees of stealing, and this kind doesn't count at all.*

She harrumphs, keeps casting judgment with her eyes. I ignore her.

Howl is Matt's dog, one of the many things he loved that he forgot to take with him when he left last year. Other items on this list include his amps, tambourines and harmonicas. All of his guitars—except for the blues guitar—as well as his entire record collection, which ranges from bluegrass, rockabilly and country to blues—both Delta and Chicago style—'60s psyche-delic, Motown, early Lower East Side punk, early British punk, grunge and electronica. And, of course, me. He found Howl one night on his way home from a jam. A huge gray mutt with human eyes. He said she had the soul of an old bluesman and named her after Howlin' Wolf, even though she's a girl dog.

Together we made Howl a bit mystical. When we needed guidance, we'd ask her and try to divine the answer. It was like What Would Jesus Do but for pagan music nerds who lacked strong parental figures.

With Matt gone, treating the dog like an oracle has lost some of its charm. Since he left I fear my sense of humor has atrophied. All my jokes are old and only made sense to him.

Loveseat lady slides closer to the floor, then all the way onto it. I wait for her to settle, then take the whole pack.

The loveseat is ugly. Itchy and orange. I don't know why we wanted it, but we saw it on the sidewalk and did. Want it, I mean. It was so heavy we couldn't go more than half a block before we had to put it down. We'd put it down until we felt we could go on and then lift it up again. Me tall and strong for my age, and him for any. That's how we carried it the whole way home.

Last thing, for real this time: a wake-up call. I tune the radio to that station that exists in between the morning news, Top 40 and total static buzz. Tune it to that and then go.

Matt was the one who told me to always steal in odd numbers. Nab one or three beers from the fridge, but never two or four. Less likely to get caught that way.

At the river I flop down where no one can see me and light a stolen smoke. Howl is above and behind me. I only leash her for the walk. She doesn't really need a leash, but I kind of like the feeling of being pulled in one solid direction.

The snow is a better bed than the one I have at home. It fits my back right, and I don't feel the cold through the fabric of my layers. I think my best thoughts here.

Or my clean, clear thoughts. The ones I think at other places are all muddy.

Here's a thought I've been having lately. I don't know if I believe in time. I mean, I don't believe it works for me the same way it works for other people. Other people can count on today turning into tomorrow and tomorrow turning into the day after that. But I can't count on it at all.

So I come here to collect proof that it's passing. There isn't as much as you'd think. You can see it in the sun rising above the trees on the far side of the frozen river, and in a few months, if all goes well, you'll see it in the cracks in the ice and the flowing water below. It looks like nothing is moving, but it is moving under there. It better be. In a few months the ice better crack up and the river better swell until it floods the plains surrounding the city. If it doesn't, that means this is the winter that will never end. This is the one.

This can't be the one. Because if time isn't passing, then everything is staying the same. And that would kill me. That's why I have to kill time first.

I stand up and call, "Come on, Howl! Time to wake the dead."

But she's right there behind me. Howl knows all about time. How it can stop short. Hold very still. When what you want is for it to fly. When what you want is for it to blur.

~

Our house is the one with the double yard. It gives us a certain status, though we only have it because the place next door got torched and they didn't rebuild.

When the crew came to level what the fire left, Jim took his beer outside to watch. "Thing is, Jo," he said, "you've gotta find the sweet spot. Once you do, one tap and the whole thing comes tumbling down."

Jim destroys things for a living. He and Maggie were still together then. We all were.

The day of the fire, after the trucks had left and all the neighbors had gone back inside, I snuck over to investigate. The ground was burned darker in the places where the flames had blown out the windows. I bent down to touch it, but it wasn't warm anymore like I'd wanted it to be.

I was eight. I remember because divorce was in the air. By the end of that summer Jim had moved across town. Every summer since, Maggie has dragged a barbecue home, and cracked plastic lawn chairs appear, and she and her crowd drink sweaty beers and cook hot dogs to a crisp and carry on, carry on until something dark happens to shut it down, like the sun comes up or the cops show or whatever. When the leaves change and fall all at once, the way they do here, she takes the barbecue over to the scrapyard by the tracks, where you can get ten bucks for the lid alone.

Grass never grew back in the spot where the house next door burned down. I suppose if we had planted some it might have, but we did not. We're Tuckers, and we do not build things. We only tear them down.

~

At the front door I listen. Radio still on but tuned to a single station with the volume low. Bacon in the pan. Char, Maggie's best friend, is in the kitchen. She comes over most mornings to make sure all the bodies have dispersed and that we don't stay in bed longer than we're supposed to. It's annoying, but she's not wrong. Otherwise we would both probably stay in bed.

I let Howl go, and she races ahead toward the smell. "Jo?" Char calls.

"Uh-huh," I say, shedding layers in the hall. The living room is empty—the drunks have cleared out.

"Breakfast," says Char.

"School," I say, walking into the room. Char's rat dog, Baby, is on the table, sniffing at a box of donuts. I toss her onto a chair and pour myself some coffee. Upstairs, Maggie is singing in the shower. Sounds like Shania. Maggie loves all her divas equally, but she believes she and Shania are spiritually aligned. This is based on their common roots in the poor backwoods of Northern Ontario and because they've both been dragged through the mud by evil, heartless men while maintaining relatively svelte figures and immaculate hairdos against all odds.

Char and I both relax a tad, because if Maggie's singing that means she's not too hungover. I help myself to a donut.

"Good girl," says Char. "You gonna be around tonight?"

I shake my head no.

"Me neither. I've got a date."

"Oh yeah?" I say. "Who's this week's winner?"

Char's been on an Internet dating rampage lately. It's hard to keep track.

"He's a new one. His profile says he's an entrepreneur."

I raise an eyebrow. She watches me refill my coffee. No sleep again last night.

"It's too bad you're not going to be around later," she says, all faux-casual, obviously working an angle. "Your mom could use someone to help her run through her number for karaoke. She's gotta get a high score tonight to make it to the next round."

"We'll see," I say, even though we won't. Maggie worships at the karaoke altar. It's sad, but I also get it a little. Aside from taking trips in my head, music is my favorite way to kill time, and I guess some people might call what Maggie does music. She acts like she's got a gig every week when really any old drunk can pick a song and sing it onstage. They're running a contest this month, though, *American Idol* style, with judges and shit. The rehearsals that have been going on nightly in the living room would be enough to send me into hiding, if I wasn't hiding already.

"Quarterfinals are tonight," says Char. "Competition's heating up."

I hear Maggie's phone ring upstairs. It's probably Dwayne, Maggie's long-suffering boss and unofficial benefactor of our lives. He's another one of her cousins, who for some unfathomable reason never tires of helping us out of cash-money jams. Dwayne hit the jackpot when he got into the tanning-salon business about ten years ago. Turns out fake tans are big business around here, there not being many months of the year in which to get a real one. He paid my swim club dues and for Matt's guitar lessons, not to mention the down payment on this house. Two years ago he took the plunge and gave Maggie a job. Amazingly, she generally shows up five days a week, more or less on time, thanks to Char.

Now Char sighs over her cell phone. "Maybe I need another new profile. Could you help me with it tomorrow?"

Maggie's voice moves toward the stairs. I wave my donut at Char and go down to the basement. We are trying a new thing, my Maggie and I. We don't talk except through third parties. Works great.

The Gibson is on the bed where I left it. I sit down to eat my donut before I pick it up. Howl has followed me—she doesn't really like the basement, but she likes Baby less—and she settles onto the floor and gives me this look. This look that says, *You should get ready for school.*

It's still early.

Not that early, she says, her eyes following the donut as I move it into my mouth.

I talk through crumbs. *Nothing important happens at school before 10 AM, plus I went yesterday. That should hold me for a while.*

You did not go yesterday! I know you were downtown.

I toss her the last bite of donut. She snaps her jaws and catches it easy. *Relax, man,* I say, licking the sugar from my fingers. (She hates it when I call her "man.") *School and I have reached an understanding.*

Howl sniffs. *I sure hope so.*

I know so, I say, picking up the guitar and starting to play. I just want to keep practicing the song I wrote last night.

Your E is flat, says Howl. She stands up, turns around twice and sits back down facing away from me. *And don't be a jerk. Help Char with her profile.*

She's right. The dog's got a good ear.

Char gets me to write all her dating profiles, even though I doubt my carefully curated list of musical interests is helping her get laid. I don't understand Internet dating. But then, I don't understand much of anything to do with people. If I wrote a profile for myself it'd say I reside in the frozen armpit that is the North End of Winnipeg with a semi-telepathic dog and my mother, who named me Jolene after a slutty lady in a Dolly Parton song. It would list my favorite things as sandwiches and music played at a volume that will destroy my eardrums by the time I'm twenty. My pastimes include taking my can of mace and my dog for long walks along the seedy riverbank, where in summer I can watch the mud-hued waters of the Red drift by, placid yet menacing. I used to swim competitively, but I quit last year, washed up at fifteen. Last summer I worked at a frozen-yogurt place downtown, and I think I did an okay job even though I don't speak small talk. Technically, I still work there—they just put me on call for the off-season, and they never call. My skills include being able to read the facial expressions of dogs with a high degree of accuracy, holding my breath for extended periods of time and giving my five-foot-ten-inch mother a fireman's lift up the stairs. I've read a wide array of depressing works of literature, and despite my love of loud music I've got extremely good, possibly supernatural, hearing. But I never would write an Internet dating profile for myself. So it's just more shit I'll never say out loud.

I stop to rest my fingertips. My calluses are peeling because it's winter and everyone's skin is flaking off, but also because I've been playing so much.

When Matt left, parts of me stopped working. My mouth doesn't move when I try to talk. Or it opens but nothing comes out. At night when I lie down to sleep, I can't close my eyes, even when I try. My feet won't listen to reason. Some days they insist on carrying me to a strange part of town, like they have an appointment to keep that I'm not privy to. My brain can't compute simple things. Like, I forget to listen when people talk, and sometimes it slips my mind where I am, what I'm doing, and when I wake back up to it, it's alarming.

But I can play better than I could play before. My hands do things they couldn't. My voice reaches for the note it needs. There's no thinking involved. It's something else.

Matt only took the custom-made blues guitar with him. The rest are all mine now—the little acoustic, the Gibson and good old Shredder—and I've been teaching myself how to play. I had to. Otherwise I'd only get to sing silently.

I play my song again, trying to get it perfect this time. I think it counts as a song, but I don't know how to tell when you're making more than noise, when you've given the sound enough shape to call it something else. I played it over and over last night so I wouldn't forget it. I played till it infiltrated my bones and my pulse fell in step alongside it, until I could hear it even when I stopped playing, so that any dreams I might have had were drowned out. Music is the noise I make out loud. The rest I keep inside myself.

When I stop, the house goes silent. Howl rises as I do, and I switch off the amp, then climb the stairs into daylight. Maggie and Char have both gone to work. I layer up and put my boots back on. No snow pants when I go downtown. Means cold legs, but I have my pride, you know. I pause on the front steps to let my eyes adjust. The sky is clear, and the sun on all that snow is blinding. It's February, and it feels like it'll never thaw.

TWO

Most of what they say about Winnipeg is true. It's cold and flat. When it's not cold it's flooding or burning down in an act of arson, or someone is being knifed in a back lane as a swarm of mosquitoes feast on the flesh of victim and assailant alike. But it always persists in being profoundly, devastatingly flat.

The flatness is almost unchallenged. There is only a handful of high-rise buildings downtown, so mostly what you notice here is the emptiness and, above you, the sky.

That'd be the third thing of note about Winnipeg. We have an abundance of sky, so much I think we could sell some of it off and still have a surplus. It really doesn't seem to serve any purpose except to remind you what a blip you are in the grand old scheme of things.

Here is what I know of this place.

The city is cut in two by a train yard. Predictably, there's a right and a wrong side of the tracks. We live in the North End, the wrong side, where teen moms push pudgy-cheeked

babies in rickety strollers, and corners are haunted by gang
members in their colors and hookers in their heels. Not every
stereotype is true; there are nuances, exceptions, but you also
get what you'd expect. Businesses open and close in time
with the rhythms of city-hall-speak about inner-city revitali-
zation, but only the fast-food chains seem to flourish. Over
by the tracks are the scrapyards, where you can hawk stolen
manhole covers and other precious metals. In front yards,
muscle-bound dogs test the limits of their chains until the
grass wears down to dirt.

Lots of Indigenous people live in the North End, so many
that sometimes it's called an urban reserve. We're white,
which means we live here but a lot of things that happen
here don't happen to us. Like, you know, the fallout from a
couple of centuries of racism and cultural genocide. We can
just leave the North End, and it's behind us. Char is Ojibwa,
and she says the North End follows her wherever she goes.

Two bridges go over the tracks to the right side of town,
but I'm afraid of bridges. I'm afraid of a lot of things. I work
around it.

You can also escape the North End by walking down
Main to the underpass that goes below the tracks or by taking
the path that runs along the river. That's the way I go if I don't
feel like navigating the crowds that huddle outside the hotel
beverage rooms on Main at all times of day. Lean-tos left by
last summer's hobos poke out from underneath the snow, and
sometimes you'll pass a few drinkers resting on the riverbank,
king cans between their knees. Mostly it's deserted this time

of year, except for the stuffed animals that are propped up next to a tree, a memorial for two brothers who went through the ice last year, one of them going under and the other plunging in after. No one found them until the ice cracked up a couple of weeks later.

This winter has been the coldest on record. This winter it's been colder here than it is on Mars. That's a true fact—they keep repeating it on TV. Everyone here watches the Weather Channel. It validates our suffering somehow.

Usually winter is quiet, what with the sun going down by four, but this year it's so dead you can't even imagine. But try. Imagine air so cold bare skin freezes in less than sixty seconds. Imagine a horror movie where the entire city you live in is trying to kill you. Everyone stays locked up tight in their homes, afraid to go outside. That's what this winter has been like.

Except for me. I go out. I do it all the time.

⌒

King's Cash for Gold is my favorite pawnshop, hands down. Don't be fooled by the name—they deal in much more than gold. Behind the thick, yellowed glass of the front window is a wide array of the kind of junk no one ever buys. A coat rack and a pinball machine. A collection of old license plates, pool cues and an eight-track player. The massive head of a moose who's misplaced one eye. Shelves of movies and CDs spill over into milk crates on the floor, board games from bygone eras

lurk underneath tables, and a portrait of the Queen presides
over it all.

The stuff people trade in for fast cash is fascinating. Most
of this shit has been here since I was a kid. Electronics and
instruments seem to be all that ever sells. Everything else just
sits around accumulating dust, including Earl, who glances
up when I come in, blinks and turns back to the stereo he's
tinkering with. For all the attention he pays, I could be the
wind. It's the relationship I've built with Earl over the years
that keeps me coming back.

I haven't been by yet this week, but there's nothing new
except for a pretty blond acoustic. I slip behind the counter
and reach for it. Earl gave me behind-the-counter privileges a
while back. He got tired of me coming in to ogle the guitars.
Must figure it runs in the family.

The first time Matt and I came to King's it was to buy the
TV back after Maggie pawned it to acquire funds for a bottle
of Canadian Club, one of the really massive bottles they keep
locked up on a special shelf at the liquor store.

"You guys aren't thinking about this logically," she said
when we protested. "It's an investment. By buying one big
bottle instead of all those little ones, I'll save enough for three
TVs by the end of the month."

I don't know how long I play—there are no clocks in here,
and Earl doesn't care. Like I said, music helps me pass the
time. Sometimes I play for what I think is five minutes when
in fact it's been an hour. Sometimes I come up from the basement and two days have passed.

Eventually I put the acoustic back in its place on the wall. It's a nice guitar, but all wrong. Earl's given up on my ever buying one of the guitars I ogle, but I do want to. It's just that I'm looking for something in particular.

If I think about it too hard, I start feeling really bad for the pawnshop guitars. You know their owners loved them once, but then they fucked up and had to make a desperate move, or else the guitar got old and they craved something better or different or both. Like a lot of things that make me sad, I try not to think about it.

There are also times when I pester Earl with questions. That's how I know our DVD player could buy me a bus ticket as far as Virden. Add the TV to that, and I'd make it to Swift Current. My iPod would get me to Lethbridge, and the gold ring from Maggie's ex, the one we called Sideburn Guy, that might take me all the way to the coast, but Earl said he'd have to see it to say for sure.

~

At the university I buy a large carton of chocolate milk in the cafeteria and sit on a bench at the bottom of the escalators to drink it. The school is made up of a bunch of little buildings scattered over a couple of downtown blocks, connected by walkways so you don't have to go outside. People are big on not going outside around here.

Several of these buildings connect in a hub of activity by the escalators, with passersby coming from five or six directions. It's one of the best places to go unnoticed. Sometimes I read or write in my notebook, but mostly I just watch. I like the bustle—everyone is going somewhere, not like at my high school, where they're all just hanging around.

My milk carton is empty by the time I spot a target. Young guy, probably first year. He wears wire-rimmed glasses and dark clothes all faded from the wash. I hop on the escalator a few steps behind him, noting the thin paperback he's got tucked under one arm. I've gotten pretty good at being able to tell chemistry students from psych students from theater students. I trail him into a lecture hall and grab a seat at the back. In the aisle in front of me a girl pulls books out of her bag. I catch sight of a title. Atwood. That'll do.

See, the thing is, I do go to school. Just not my school. At least, no more than I have to.

~

Class ends, and I wait for my row of seats to clear. The guy next to me is taking his sweet time packing up, so I fuss with my iPod since I can't slip around him.

The lecture was good. Oddly enough, the topic was winter as theme in literature. I hadn't read the books they were talking about, so I had to infer a lot—like overhearing a phone call on the bus and filling in the gaps—but I didn't mind. It pushes you, being in over your head. Swimming was like that. I'd get moved to a higher group, and the workouts would be so tough it was like every practice was an exercise in trying not to drown. As soon as I'd realize I wasn't clinging to the side of the pool after each set of sprints anymore, I'd get moved up and be drowning all over again. It happened time after time, like clockwork, so I almost didn't realize how fast I was getting. Playing guitar is like that too. Every so often I'll notice I can do something with ease that I always fumbled before.

I put my headphones on and start my music as buddy beside me gets his act together and moves into the aisle. I'm shuffling toward the door when I realize a girl is talking to me. She has pale purple hair, and her hand is on my arm. "Tucker?"

I try to go blank-faced as students flow around us down the aisle. I want to flow with them, out onto the street and away from this, but she's in the way and beaming at me. I take my headphones off.

"I thought I saw you last week! By the escalators. You had headphones on and didn't hear me. I'm Ivy, from swimming? I didn't know you were in this fucking class!"

I remember her as a real live wire, running across the pool deck before a race, whipping butts with a towel and sending the lifeguards reaching for their whistles. She was a bit older than me and swam for one of the big teams in the south end, but we went up against each other all the time. Once she came to a meet hungover and puked in the pool during warm-up. They had to postpone the races while they drained all the water or added more chemicals or whatever they do.

I mumble something to the tune of hey, how's it going, and she laughs. Looks at me close, with all these questions, and I know I've got to get away. I start toward the door, but she stays with me. I can't lose her, just like in the pool. What she says isn't what I expect her to. "I wasn't surprised when you quit, you know."

The hall is crammed with classes letting out, and we're stuck in a pack moving toward the street. Nowhere to run. "You weren't?"

"No way, man. I could tell you were never really into it."

"I wasn't?" This is news to me. I spent years churning chlorinated water, trying to go fast. I wanted to be faster than her, faster than everyone else, faster than myself.

"Nah. I mean, you were pretty good, but I could tell you didn't live for it."

"I guess not." How do you live for something anyway? What does that feel like?

"So what do you do now?"

"Umm." I stall, half figuring out how to answer her question, half plotting how I'm going to lose her.

"Like, what do you do now instead of swimming? I bet you draw or act or volunteer somewhere, something more interesting than swimming back and forth staring at the bottom of a pool seven days a week, right?"

"I guess I'm learning to play the guitar."

"I knew it!" We're outside now, but she doesn't seem to notice the cold, taking her time shoving her arms into the sleeves of her jacket, not letting it interrupt her talk. "It's like, when you quit, suddenly there's all this time and space to do that kinda stuff. It's like your idea of who you are totally shifts, because what are we if we're not what we do, right? I've gotten really into my art. I can't believe I spent so long pretending to be a jock. My dad pretty much cried when I quit. He was hoping for scholarships. Hey, I should show you some of my stuff sometime. Which way are you going?"

We're about to cross the street to where I'd catch my bus, but I stop and point back at school. "I forgot something."

"Oh," she says. "I guess I'll see you in class then."

No she won't.

⌒

Matt got his driver's license the moment he turned sixteen. At the time, Maggie had a boyfriend with a car and no life who took her anywhere she needed to go. That left us with her Chrysler LeBaron. Rust spread like a nasty rash across its pale yellow paint. It was a car that could not be killed, no matter what you did. Maggie forgot to renew the insurance, but we called it the Illegal Mobile and drove it anyway.

We found all kinds of reasons to get in the car. For a while our favorite thing was to drive out to the airport, pay the three bucks to park, and sit at the arrival gates, watching people come down the escalators. It made me feel sophisticated, being at the airport, having never gone anywhere. And it was kind of uplifting to see people look so happy to be in Winnipeg. You don't see it that much. We'd eat fast food and watch the arrivals hug their loved ones, pluck their bags off the carousel and head home. Matt would let me have sips of his coffee, and I'd go motor-mouthed, telling him everything there was of my world, which was school, swimming and nothing else. He, in turn, would tell me stories about great musicians, about Neil Young, Joe Strummer and Howlin' Wolf. Sometimes I'd be in bed already, and he'd show up at my bedroom door and say, *Wanna go to the airport?* And off we'd go.

⁓

After ditching Ivy, I duck into the Greyhound station next door to the university. There are no smiling faces to greet you here, just a piss-smelling room full of desperate folks sleeping one off or staring at the walls or otherwise wasting away.

It's too early to go home, so I decide to stay a while.

Mullet lady is working the ticket counter. She's my favorite. She doesn't seem to have the ability to smile. I like to be nice to her and watch it freak her out. I'm not in that particular mood today though. Too shaken up by my run-in with Ivy.

I started skipping school to hang out at the university last year. I liked the way it was full of people who didn't know me, who didn't notice me either. One day I was walking down the hall and followed the flow of traffic into a classroom. It was a big room, full of people, and I still felt invisible, so I sat down, stayed. I listened to the lecture. In the fall it became a habit, going downtown and finding a classroom to sit in. Sometimes I listened, and sometimes it wasn't about listening. It was more the feeling I was after. That I was someone else. Now my cover's blown.

Another habit of mine is watching the 9:50 westbound bus leave the terminal. The one Matt took. I like to entertain the thought of getting on it too.

Matt left while I was sleeping. No goodbye, just a note for me in the basement. It didn't say anything worth repeating. Just that there was a Greyhound sale. Just that he was going to go west and have an adventure. Just that he'd be back in a few weeks. I'd never known him to lie before.

To cheer myself up, I go talk to mullet lady at the ticket desk. "How much for a ticket to Victoria?"

"Round trip or one way?" she counters, like she always does. And like I always do, I balk because it's such a big question, but then I say one way, because it's easiest, and it's what he would have said. She punches something into her computer. "Two hundred and forty-seven dollars after taxes. You wanna hear the round-trip total too?"

"No thanks." I pull on my hat and walk out into the street.

See, I have this theory that leaving is a muscle. I'm trying to work mine out.

THREE

The front window flashes with strange light as I walk up the path. I regard it warily.

Inside, the living room has been transformed into a jazz lounge. Or is it a dive bar? Maybe it's the saddest rave in the world. Hard to say.

A haze of cigarette smoke obscures the room, but not nearly enough. The furniture has been pushed aside, and the lights are low and pulsing—Maggie has hooked up the strobe light Matt and I bought at a garage sale years ago. Roxie is on the couch, painstakingly applying rhinestones to her fingernails. Char's by the window, a bottle of wine at her feet. She's munching on a bowl of peanuts in the shell, feeding some to Baby one at a time. And Maggie's center stage, her back to me, hair teased into a lopsided beehive, holding on to a high note for dear life.

I blink. Is this what a bad acid trip is like?

Maggie raises her arms for the finale, brandishing her karaoke mic like it's the Olympic torch. She's too lost in song to notice me. Char and Roxie clap obediently. I drop my bag, take off my boots and head for the kitchen with Howl at my heels.

Cory's at the counter, pouring himself a drink. "Hey, Jo," he says. "Want a shot?"

"No thanks," I say. Cory is yet another member of the Tucker clan to be proud of. I once saw him actually attempt to eat glass. Not even on a dare. Another time he wore a pair of shoes so small that every last one of his toenails fell off. Then he didn't go to the doctor, and his nail beds were oozing bright-green pus. Like spearmint toothpaste, he said.

I stare into the fridge for a while, then check the freezer and find a frozen dinner some forward-thinking genius (me) purchased and hid beneath plastic bags of bread ends, ice-cube trays and bottles of vodka. It's not that we're poor, per se. Maggie likes to claim we're part of the creative class, though what the fuck she means by that I do not know. What I do know is we have enough to smoke and drink and eat, in that order.

I'm punching buttons on the microwave when a throat clears behind me.

I ignore it, but it comes again.

I take my time turning around.

Among Maggie's many talents is the ability to give a profoundly unnerving stinkeye. This is a look that makes government officials bend, men blubber like babies and sales-people put in calls to their managers. I wish I could say that I inherited it, but all I seem to have gained from my Tucker genetic material is the inability to integrate into normal society.

"Oh, hey," I say.

"*Oh, hey*," she says back in scary singsong, her hand moving to her hip as she assumes bitch stance. Cory downs his shot and shifts uncomfortably. "Make any long-distance phone calls lately?" she says. It's not a question. She tosses an envelope at me. It falls to the floor, and I bend to retrieve it. It's the bill for my phone, which I am supposed to pay and which I have not paid in over five months. Meaning I've fallen a bit behind. Like, four hundred dollars behind.

"Oh shit."

"Oh shit indeed," says Maggie.

"Sorry?"

"Hand it over."

Cory slips out of the room with his bottle. I gaze long-ingly after him as I reach into my pocket and give her my phone. It's not like anyone ever calls me anyway.

"Good," she says, pleased with my obedience. "Now get a job." She turns on one kitten heel, the pink-feathered pair she's been favoring lately.

"I have a job," I say, but she's already gone. "Sort of."

"Well," she yells from the hallway, "get another one."

You have to be quick with Maggie. She'll take off on a whim and leave you behind. Once when I was nine she left me at the Dairy Queen in Dryden for three hours. The girl behind the counter told me if I washed her dishes at the end of the night she'd let me sleep in her backyard.

"Let's go," Maggie says to the living room crowd. Cory and Roxie follow her out the front door, while Char scrambles to get her and Baby's jackets on.

"Don't worry," she says, shoving Baby's furry limbs through the sleeves of his ridiculous dog parka. "She'll cool down."

"What happened to your date?"

"Oh," Char calls over her shoulder, "he canceled." And then they're gone.

I sit down, and Howl puts her head on my knee, looking for all the world like she knows every stupid thing I do, including, but not limited to, hiding the phone bill for the last five months in the sleeve of a Patti Smith record. Usually I'm careful to intercept the mail before Maggie gets to it. Maybe it's the lack of sleep making me messy, or maybe I was more shaken up by Ivy recognizing me than I thought. Either way, I have to pay attention, or bad things will happen.

The microwave beeps, but I ignore it and hook the leash onto Howl's collar. Not hungry anymore. The way Howl is looking at me makes me queasy with guilt. Maybe this is what it's like having a mom who doesn't disappear for three days to go hot-tubbing with a guy she met at bingo. I'm not used to disappointing anyone except myself.

I knew it was a stupid thing to do, I tell Howl. *It's not like I expected the bill to go away. I just kind of thought I might.*

Did you go to school today? she asks as I put my boots on.

Sort of.

So no then?

Don't.

It just defies logic, is all. That a girl who claims to want out of here so badly, but won't leave until she's done high school, would fail to do the things she needs to do in order to graduate. It's almost like she doesn't actually want to leave.

Ha! Keep dreaming.

Well, how do you explain it then?

Explain what?

Your behavior.

I groan. *Maybe your dog brain can't compute it, but lots of things aren't logical, Howl. Not just me and my truancy.*

She goes to wait for me at the front door. I've done it now. Whatever. She pushed my buttons too. I'm well aware my actions don't support my escape plans. I should either shut up and finish high school or shut up and leave already. But I'm too scared to just get up and go without any savings or so much as a high school diploma. And I'm no good at making myself do things I don't want to do, such as attending high school. I wake up in Winnipeg every day. That's bad enough.

~

Back to the river we go. Howl romps and sniffs and hunts while I lie down and let the snow hold me. The sky is clouded over, and I pick out shapes in the naked treetops. I see a woman bent double, and I see a hooded figure walking tightrope, and I see skeleton hands reaching for the moon.

Theoretically the Earth will do one more lap around the sun, and then it'll be time. My time. Time to go. That's why I'm working out my leaving muscle.

I watch the snow drifting to the ground, taking its sweet time. It covers me slowly, until I'm camouflaged completely.

Sometimes I think I might die of exposure.

FOUR

I walk home and into the kind of quiet that makes the house double over in silence. It rings through my ears, the rooms and everything. I wander through the first floor, picking up debris. Bottle caps and rhinestones, lipstick, high heels that didn't make the cut, and all kinds of empties. An unsmoked cigarette rests on the edge of the ashtray in the kitchen. I light it and take a drag. Ever since Matt left, Maggie fills the house with people. She did it before he left too, but there's a big difference between bringing the bar home because you don't want the party to end and because you don't want to walk into the house and hear nothing. It's true that if we didn't manufacture so much noise, there would be none.

I retrieve the once-frozen dinner from the microwave, eat it mechanically, then go upstairs to bed. Maggie doesn't like me sleeping in the basement—says it creeps her out. Considering our argument, I figure I'm due for a show of good behavior.

But I can tell right away sleep isn't going to come. When I was still swimming, I fell asleep every night no problem. I slept right through the sound of Matt's guitar coming up through the vent, through Maggie bringing home friends from the bar after last call. Now sleep escapes me. Now I wake up every time the windowpane beside my bed rattles in the wind. I wake up every time footsteps disturb the fallen snow outside. Every time the dog sighs downstairs in the dark.

I roll over and pound the lumps out of my pillow. Howl's tags clink, and her face appears, cold, wet nose on mine. I get up and go downstairs, then down again to the basement.

The air smells of wet cement and teenage boy, even though only Howl and I hang around here these days. It's cold, so I turn the space heater on and sit down on the bed. Howl settles onto the floor beside me.

Our basement is haunted by the ghosts of rock 'n' roll, among other things. Matt covered the walls with posters of his gods—Kurt Cobain and Leadbelly hang out above a stack of amps, while Johnny Cash and Jimi Hendrix and Joe Strummer are lined up on the wall next to me. In the dim lamplight their faces come alive. "Hey, guys. How's life?" I say.

But they don't answer. The quiet gets louder. I grab a guitar and drown it out.

~

Maggie comes home before last call. She's not alone, but almost. There's a man too. I track her movements through the floor. She goes to the kitchen first, opens the fridge, closes it again and continues on upstairs, giggling. I can tell by the way she stops in the bathroom to take her makeup off that she's drunk but not wasted. She'll get up in the morning.

I switch off the amp, and the warm buzz of it drains out of the air. I lie down on Matt's old single bed in the corner and try to stop my ears from searching.

Once, Jim's demolition company had this job tearing the safe out of the basement of a bank downtown. The work could only be done after all the other offices in the building were empty. Night after night, Jim went down and used this giant jackhammer to chip away at the thing, trying to break it into pieces so they could remove it from the building. It took weeks. The job went way over budget. No one expected the safe would be so hard to destroy.

When I can't sleep at night because of the drunks or Maggie crying or any of the other sounds I can't help but be attuned to, I think about Jim working away downtown underground, trying to destroy something that was meant to last forever. I really admire that kind of blind commitment to a goal. Maybe that's why I used to love swimming back and forth, staring at the bottom of a pool, for so many hours every day. It's the same thing with Maggie believing she's going to be a famous singer when she grows up, even though she's an alcoholic tanning-salon manager with middle-aged spread and next to no singing ability whatsoever. Yet her faith in herself never seems to falter.

I wish I could still believe in stupid, impossible things like that. But I seem to have lost the knack for it.

After a while I can't take the quiet, so I drag the space heater over to the bed. It's the kind that shuts off after a few minutes and then automatically turns back on when the room cools again. Every time the low murmur of the fan cuts out, quiet invades my ears and I reach over and pump it up to a higher setting, then a higher one still. Eventually it gets so hot I throw the blankets back and tear my pajamas off, so I'm lying in my underwear next to a panting dog, trying my fucking hardest not to hear how silent it is behind the whirl of the heater. Because when it's not too loud around here, it's far too quiet.

FIVE

Third period. English with Ms. Groves. The best thing about Groves is all her facial expressions. She doesn't hide the hate. She's doing that thing where she waits for the class to stop talking. Just looks at us and waits. You can totally tell she's judging the alpha girls by the door sighing over their cell phones, or the dude in the sports-themed clothing reciting a list of everything he drank last night to no one in particular, or the girl in front of me who's pulled out a small pair of scissors and begun to meticulously snip her split ends one hair at a time, a process she will keep up for the whole class. Groves just sits there watching, and then after a while people realize she's giving them a stinkeye that rivals my mother's, and they quiet the fuck down. It's kind of amusing. Not quite reason enough to show up for class, but almost.

The classroom falls silent, and Groves lets the silence go until it's good and awkward. "All right," she says. "Who wants to read today? I need an Orlando? A Duke? An Adam?

Who wants Adam? Anyone?" She rattles off roles like a bored auctioneer. Hands go up.

She scares the teenagers, she does, because she doesn't abide by the rules of high school. She'll find you smoking behind the Dumpsters if you don't show up for class. She'll call your house and read your essay on *Gatsby* out loud to your mother to illustrate that she's raised a dummy.

I sit quietly, eyes front, as roles are handed out. We have an agreement, Groves and I. Well, we have a few of them. She won't make me talk in class, and I'll keep coming to class. I find if you cultivate an aura of pathological quietness, most teachers will leave you alone in the end.

"All right," says Groves. "Let's go."

Here's the secret to how I survive school: I'm not really here. Even when I am here, I'm not. Every morning before I come inside, I take my real self by the hand, walk her to a room at the back of my mind and softly close the door. Then I go through the motions of the day. But I'm not here really. Really, I'm far away.

The bell tolls lunch, and bodies fly out of the room while Groves is still assigning the homework for next class. I close my books and wait for the last of the stragglers to clear. Groves erases the chalkboard in big sweeping motions, leaving half the letters behind. I stand up and sit down again, this time at the desk right in front of hers.

Here's the deal with Groves. She watches and makes sure I stay. I know—creepy, right? Not actually though. She's a bit lame but pretty cool in the grand scheme. She pays attention like I do. Not many people pay attention these days. Everyone just goes around so careless.

I don't go to the airport anymore because of Groves. For a while I was taking the bus out there to watch the departures. I'm not so into arrivals anymore. She saw me there one time and thought it was weird and made kind of a thing out of it. So I'm not supposed to go there anymore. She doesn't know about the bus station. She thinks I get all my leave-taking talk out with her and doesn't know I'm only partly holding up my end. Her end is she keeps the school from kicking me out, which is an idea they were floating for a while. My end is I do research and extra essays and talk when I'd rather not. She asks me weird questions like, *where are the women in Ginsberg's poems?* and *what do you dream of when you dream of the future?* I try to make up some junk to tell her other than the truth, which is that I don't dream, not the good kind anyway, but sometimes I slip and find myself telling her something true. Too true. The kind of truth you should keep to yourself.

"So where are we going today?" she asks, flipping on the electric kettle she keeps by the window before sitting down at her desk.

"I was thinking Alberta maybe. Like, in the mountains."

"Oh God, don't go there."

"Why not?"

"Because why would you go somewhere worse than here? Where's the sense in that?"

"What's worse about it?" I ask. And then we look for evidence. Groves is big on evidence. She says we can't just go around believing in magic and nonsense and any old thing. She says beliefs have to be supported by research and facts and proof. She says I can't leave because I think it'll be better somewhere else. That's the other part of our deal. If I stay until I graduate next year, she says she'll help me find a good way out. I think that anywhere but here is good enough, but she says I'm not thinking, I'm feeling. I don't know about that. I don't know if things make as much sense as she tries to make of them. I think there's more chaos to it than that.

The kettle boils, and she makes us tea while we talk cost of living and marketable skills and she asks me, "What about winter?" and "Do you like cowboys?" Because apparently there are cowboys there. Or like, bros in cowboy hats. She says that and then I ask her for some proof, and she's all like, "I lived in Banff in 1998 and it was the worst summer of my life." What was worst about it? I ask. And she tells me about the guy she moved out there for and her crappy waitressing job and how all the bars played country music and something about crabs and that doesn't sound like proof to me, but it gets her talking and then she forgets about making me talk. So I'm not going to argue with her.

After a bit her rant winds down, and she starts in on a sales pitch for this university on the east coast she thinks I should apply to, which is where these talks always land.

It's also where I tune out, because I don't have any goals except getting out of here alive and maybe one day becoming a famous recluse or studying the art of the mixtape, and neither of those pursuits requires a university education.

"So," she says, shutting up at last, "what do you think?"

This is what happens when people ask me what I'm thinking: all my thoughts go kamikaze and commit suicide. They evaporate into the thin air inside my mind. But I know she won't break the silence until I say something, so I say, "I hate it here."

"That's the spirit." She nods like this is a reasonable contribution to the conversation, takes out a sandwich and offers half to me. I take it, having made the mistake of refusing it before. Is it bad that I'm not even worried about being seen eating lunch with a teacher? This school is big, but not big enough that no one knows me. I think my plan to disappear is working though. This is another, older plan. It involves ignoring the whispers that sometimes still follow me down the hall. I've been here three years now, and people know me less and less all the time. It goes both ways. Names I used to know I've been forgetting. I wear my headphones in the halls, and the music makes a wall around me. Groves is the only one who tries to get around it.

After we're done chewing and I've spent several minutes playing with crumbs, I say, "I need to find a new job."

Groves nods. "Don't we all!" The bell rings, and I grab my bag. "I'll let you know if I hear of anything," she says as I go.

~

Bio lets out last period and there's a crush for the doors. It's Friday, and everyone is hungry to get out of here, including me, though I'm also just hungry. In the hall I fight my way upstream to my locker, dump my books, layer up and make for the stairs, dreaming of the leftovers I'll reheat when I get home. Yes, heat up leftovers and crawl into bed. Howl's walk can wait until later. I chart a course across the main hall toward the back doors. I tend to come and go through the staff parking lot, cutting across the field behind the school and avoiding human contact, if you can call my cohorts human, which I don't. Groves and Vice-Principal Lambert are lurking outside the gym, though, so instead I enter the stream of students headed out the front doors, since it's entirely possible my favorite authority figures are talking about me.

The street in front of the school is bottlenecked with traffic—parents picking up their kids and students idling their cars, windows rolled down even though it's bitter out.

If it hadn't been for swimming, I would have ended up at the high school two blocks from home, which boasts a day care for students with kids and tiny class sizes beyond tenth grade because of the high dropout rate. Instead, I wound up out in the suburbs at Assiniboine Collegiate because it's close to the pool I used to train at. I guess I could have transferred when I quit the team, but would it be any different at another school? I don't know. I doubt it. My peers may be hockey-breathing lower life forms, but better the lower life form you know than the one you don't. Right?

In ninth grade I made the mistake of telling some people I live in the North End. The questions that followed (*Do you, like, live below the poverty line?*) quickly taught me to gloss over that and a great many other facts of my existence.

~

In my sleep I hear singing. I'm upright before I'm even awake, wrapping a blanket around myself. "*Stop! In the name of love!*" Maggie shouts tunelessly. I take the basement stairs two at a time and find Howl waiting by the front door. We're well trained for such middle-of-the-night moments. The objective is to get her inside before she wakes the neighborhood, whose residents love nothing more than a messy boulevard drama. I drop the blanket and put on my jacket, shove my feet into a pair of boots and go outside to see what I can do.

She's teetering up the path, jacket half-draped over her shoulders, too drunk to recognize the cold. Her heels, a four-inch pair she can barely walk in at the best of times, are forcing her ankles out at a sickening angle. Where is Char? Maggie grins when she sees me, opens her arms and croons, "*Think it o-o-ver.*"

"Come on, Maggie," I say. "Let's go inside."

The grin just spreads wider, and she aims her awful eyes at me. She tries to bat her lashes, but it seems a tremendous effort. Maggie has these amazing eyes—everyone says so.

Like bright, wet chocolate, with the kind of lashes most women can't get without glue. They're her moneymaker, her God-given gift, her get-outta-jail-free card. It's pathetic, the way people get lost in those eyeballs. Not me though. I'm long since immune. Maybe she can sense that, because she gives up, and her gaze slides over me before coming to rest at a spot on the ground, where it slips out of focus.

"Maggie!" I say again. "It's late. You'll catch cold."

"It's late, you'll catch cold," she parrots, snapping back to attention. "Stop acting eighty, hon."

The black tube of her skirt has crept up her thighs while the crotch of her panty hose has worked its way down. Her lipstick is wandering across her face, and her hair, piled high in a beehive, sags to one side, like a building whose foundation is in need of repair. The hair and the heels add enough inches to her already considerable height to make her truly a giant, larger than life. She hums to herself and sways. I hurry forward as she crumbles to the ground just shy of the stairs.

I try to haul her back up, but she swats me away.

"Let me help you!" I say.

This seems to anger her. She takes a swipe at my feet and knocks me down. We lie tangled up for a moment before the struggle resumes. Finally I get her off me and pull myself onto the steps. "For fuck's sake! Stay there then!"

She plunks down next to me and takes out her smokes. I try to get up and go inside, but she grabs my ankle, says, "Sit. Wait with me."

I obey. Drunk-Maggie will not be denied.

With heavy, uncooperative hands, she lights a cigarette. "You know what your problem is, Jolene? You're too serious."

"I am."

"That's right," she slurs. "And you don't know how to have fun."

"Also true." I take the pack she holds out to me. It's dog-eared from being along for the ride on the sort of night that culminates in a grown woman serenading herself with the classic hits of Motown on an otherwise quiet street at two in the morning. She flicks her lighter, and I lean into the flame. For a moment our eyes meet, and she looks clear, she looks like my mother. But then we both break away and sit together smoking under a sky laden with stars.

Every so often, through some drunken alchemy I don't claim to understand, a change comes over Maggie, and she's stripped of her bullshit, her agendas, her plays for attention and sympathy. Her never-ending scramble to get drunk or high or otherwise altered. Every so often she drops the act, and it's like she forgets she doesn't like me and I don't like her, and we're sort of, for a lack of a better word, friends. Sure, it's always two shakes before she blacks out, but still, in these moments it is possible to have a real conversation with my mother. There on the front steps, with the frozen concrete numbing my ass, head swimming with smoke, I get the feeling it's one of those times. But how to know for sure? And what to say?

"What are we waiting for?" I ask eventually. The silence following my question goes on and on, long enough for me to consider whether or not I really want to know the answer. Her legs, shadowed in sheer black tights, had been splayed across the steps, as if she was trying to take up as much space as possible, but now she gathers them in and rests her head on her knees. "Maggie?" The cigarette is still clutched between her fingers, ash inching up toward the filter. "What are we waiting for?" I ask again.

"Louie went to get burgers. I'm *starving*."

"Oh." And then a few moments later, "Who's Louie?"

"My boyfriend," she says, like, *duh*.

"Oh," I say again. In my mother's eyes, all men are potential boyfriends. Anyone from her catalog of exes can have his status renewed, if only in conversation. The delivery guy at the twenty-four-hour pizza place is her boyfriend. The dude on the entertainment-news show is her boyfriend.

"He's nice," she says. "A nice one for once." She sits up and looks at me. "You'll hate him though. You hate everyone."

"Pretty much."

She seems pleased I'm siding with her on this one. "You've always been a bit weird, my girl."

"Hmm."

She stands up and peers down the street like she sees someone coming. I stand too and try to stop her as she flops down in the deep snow beyond the path. "What're you doing? Come on, Maggie. Get up." I grab her arm and pull so hard I'm afraid I'll dislocate it. She doesn't budge. I let it drop.

"Come on," she says. "Come make a snow angel with your mom."

I lie down next to her, but neither of us moves our legs or our arms, so we're not really making angels at all. "You wouldn't play with other kids," she goes on. "You'd hang back and study the game until you'd gathered enough information in your little brain, and then you'd play. I worried about you. You seemed so afraid. I've always worried about you. I never worried about Matt."

"Shut up," I say, but not as meanly as I might. This is nothing she hasn't said before. When we were growing up, Matt had to bring me everywhere because she was always out. But he never acted like it was an obligation. I'd forget that I was a tagalong little sister until Maggie reminded me. *Oh, she's shy,* she'd explain to strangers. *She didn't even talk until she was almost four. I took her to doctors, thought something was wrong. But she's not stupid, just quiet. Except around her brother, my oldest. Around him she talks a blue streak.* And I would cower behind her and let her explain for me. Until I got too tall and had to figure out different ways of making myself small.

She was right and wrong. I don't like talking unless I have something really good to say. And I am afraid of doing things I've never done before. I do hang back and watch. But I was different around Matt, away from her. He made me cool. Even I believed it.

There's no wind, and above us the ghost in the tree rotates slightly where it hangs over the path. "Remember that?" I say, pointing up at it.

"Yep," she says, and we watch it together, remembering.

A car pulls up, and we both struggle to get to our feet. A man I've never seen before gets out, arms laden with paper-bag fast food, grease spreading quickly across the brown.

"*Salut.*" He nods at me politely and, seeing the state Maggie's in, puts the bags down and picks her up easily, like it ain't no thing. She giggles in his arms, and they disappear inside. A moment later this Louie comes back out for the food. "Do you want some French fries?" he asks. His voice is accented, his English careful. I wonder if she told him I'm her roommate, or a local stray. Maybe all he knows how to say is "Do you want some French fries?"

I shake my head until he goes. Howl presses into me, and I put my arm around her. *We'll go inside in a minute, girl.*

I used to find our front-yard ghost amusing, then ominous, and now I'm just used to it. It was one of Maggie's whims. She decided last minute that she wanted to decorate the yard for Halloween, and, with Char's help, rigged up a ghost from an old basketball and a bedsheet, drawing a face on with mascara.

I watched from behind a book as they summoned Matt from the basement and coerced him into climbing the tree. We all filed outside to watch. The street was filling with costumed kids running about semi-supervised as their parents cracked beers and dumped candy into bowls. Matt and I had often climbed the tree when we were young. I never got much higher than the fork in the trunk, but Matt could climb way up into the branches. If nothing else, the North End is rich in trees, mostly oaks and elms, thick-trunked giants that line the streets and shade the yards. Whether they're a tangle of naked branches in winter or in full, lush summer glory, it's a relief to have something between you and the sky. People are frightened of the sky here. Or they should be.

Matt climbed the tree in long, practiced motions, grabbing on to knots he'd held countless times before. Soon he was high above us, calling down, "Where do you want it?"

Maggie and Char egged him into climbing higher, and he did, ascending to where the branches began to bend deeply under his weight. We stood silent, heads craned back as he moved out along a branch, grasping the ghost by its neck like he was its captor. He tested his weight one foot at a time, going beyond where he reasonably needed to, like he was trying to prove something.

"That's good enough!" I said, but not loudly enough for him to hear. I held my breath the whole time it took for Matt to tie the ghost up tight and inch back down, moving confidently again when he reached the solid lower branches.

We cheered when his feet hit the ground. Up and down the street, people turned. It did look great, the stark white of the sheet standing out against the trees above us, the ghost dancing this way and that in the wind.

"I knew it'd look good up there," said Maggie, puffing on a smoke.

"Your mom's got a good eye," Char said. A vampire and a gorilla hauling pillowcases of loot raced up our path, shouting, "Trick or treat!" with unchecked glee.

"Sorry, kids, no candy," Maggie said.

"You didn't get candy?" Matt asked.

"Go to that yellow house down the street!" Char said, snapping her gum. "They're giving out full-size bags of Hickory Sticks." She turned to Maggie. "Jarvis stole 'em off the back of the delivery truck." They roared with laughter.

Matt and I went out to buy some candy. By the time we got back, the trick-or-treating had slowed, so we sat on the front steps and ate ourselves sick on Rockets and Tootsie Rolls as the ghost swung back and forth above us.

The next day it snowed, and it was too dangerous for Matt to climb up and cut the ghost down. By springtime my brother was gone. So it stayed, our funny front-yard ghost, because I couldn't climb that high even if I tried.

SIX

It must be hereditary, the low-life gene, because as soon as I start thinking about how to make some money, my mind goes to pawning and pushing. Matt would kill me. He's not here, though, so I run through a list of things I could hawk in my head. The guitars, but that's not an option. I could sell some of my books, my vinyl, but at two bucks here, three bucks there, it's not worth the trouble. I could beg Cory to give me an ounce of weed on credit, but being a drug dealer requires people skills I sure as shit don't have.

Four hundred bucks. A lot of money for someone who has none. And I don't just need to pay off the phone bill. When I leave I'm going to need a chunk of change. A pretty serious chunk.

Who am I kidding? I'm not a criminal. I lack the self-confidence required to break laws. But I'm able-bodied and hardworking. I can get a new job.

Even though they haven't called me in the last six months, I swing by the frozen-yogurt stand anyway. Rhonda, the manager, is behind the counter, flipping through a gossip magazine. She keeps a stack of them beside the till. She squeals when she sees me.

"*Jolene!* How *are* you?"

"I'm okay."

"Yeah? School's good? Family doing all right?"

"Yup, stuff's good." Rhonda knows Maggie and has a tabloid-like fascination with my mother's messiness. She's always fishing for a new Maggie story. "I was wondering, do you think you'll have any shifts for me coming up?"

"Shit, sweetheart. That's a no-go, I'm afraid. We'd love to have you back in July, but things are slow as molasses right now. It's colder here than it is on Mars, you know."

"I heard. Well, thanks anyway."

"How's your mom doing?"

"Fine."

"Ya sure?"

"Pretty sure, Rhonda."

She force-feeds me a cup of piña colada and reads aloud a story about the anorexia pandemic among young Hollywood starlets. "Look how skinny that one is," she sighs.

After that I go to the library to print out a copy of my sad résumé. I actually got an A on this piece of shit for school. In order to compensate for a lack of any actual work experience, we were told to emphasize our skills. It's all lies. Am I a reliable person? Maybe. Do I have strong communication skills? Ha. Am I a team player? As a rule I do not join teams or clubs. Do I qualify as a self-starter? Perhaps, but that depends on what you need started. And when you need it started. And why. And whether I'm reading a particularly good book that day.

I walk through the mall but can't bring myself to hand out any résumés. I do try—I sit in the food court, filling out an application for the bagel place, until a security guard approaches to tell me I've exceeded the thirty-minute loitering allowance and could I please move on. They've been cracking down on food court drug deals. I leave. Didn't want a career in bagels anyway.

Outside, the streets are almost empty. Three guys huddle together in a bus shelter, passing around a bottle of Listerine, choice poison in these parts. The wind's real bad, but I pull my scarf over my face bandit style and bear it.

The professor in that class the other day said weather can be a character unto itself in literature. It moves the plot forward. It echoes what's going on in characters' lives. It interferes.

I slip, pause, and just when I get my grip on the ground, I'm sliding again. I wonder what this weather says about the novel of my life. The unsteady rhythm of my boots on the ground says *nothing good, nothing good.*

~

The familiar logo of the company sign catches my eye as I walk by, even though I've got my eyes on the ground, trying not to fall. I peer through the fence next to a sign that reads *Caution! Men Working Overhead* and don't see Jim, but I do see Gord, one of my uncles.

"Hey, Gord!" He's smoking and looking at a clipboard while some of his guys load debris into the back of a truck. "Gord!"

He looks up, yells, "Who's that?"

I stick my face up to the fence. "It's Jo. My dad around?"

"Oh, hey, Jo. He's over on the McDermot side. You want me to get him?"

"No, that's okay. I'll go find him."

"There's an entrance around the corner." He points.

"Cool. Thanks." I start in that direction.

"And put on a hard hat, you hear?"

"I will!"

It's a big job. A whole square block around an old warehouse has been fenced off. I haven't seen Jim in a couple of weeks. Last I checked, they were gutting a video store. I find the gap in the fence and go in. There's a trailer nearby, so I head there first. Jim's not in it, but I do find myself a hard hat. They had a workplace death a few years ago and since then have to be way serious about that stuff. Even Jim, who is neither safe nor serious.

I think I see him over by a truck and wave, and then I yell, "Hey, Dad!" because I realize that with the hard hat on, in my usual utilitarian winter garb, I don't look all that different from the rest of his crew. They don't call him Dad though.

"Jo! What are you doing here?"

He comes over and gives me a hug, thumping me on the back for too long.

"I was just walking by and thought I'd say hi."

"Amazing!" he practically shouts. "What a great surprise!"

We go into the trailer to get out of the cold, and he makes us hot chocolate and beams at me. "So," he says, "what's new, Champ?"

Jim is a bit tricky. I have to come up with something to tell him so he'll keep beaming, but it has to be the right thing. I can't tell him how I've slowly stopped going to school, at first because everybody looked at me and now because they don't look at me at all and it turns out maybe it's worse that way. It's what I wanted, but it's worse. I can't tell him that sometimes when I come over and we hang out, it's been a day or two since I've said much out loud, and my voice sounds strange to my ears. I can't tell him how I much I want to leave or how I'm afraid I might someday, like tomorrow or the day after that. And how I'm afraid leaving might be like other things I thought I wanted and then, after I got them, it turned out I didn't. I don't tell him how afraid I am. Of everything. How I see danger everywhere. How sometimes when I try to sleep at night I see a roof collapsing on him at work, or the floor caving in, or I see him falling. How I see Maggie plowing the car into a tree or the river or something else that seems harmless until it's not. I don't tell him how sometimes I think I'm right when I'm wrong. Really right when I'm really, really wrong. And so it's not just that I don't trust other people. I don't trust myself.

I don't tell him these things so that he won't say they're amazing. Because Jim thinks everything is amazing. And everything is not.

"Well, I like my English class, I guess. The teacher's pretty all right." I stop talking as a dude comes into the trailer, nods at us and begins to root around in the corner for something.

"Amazing! Hey, Bryan, this is my kid! She's way smarter than all of you doobs. Way too good for you too. Stop looking at her." Bryan nods and leaves, nonplussed. I think the crew is used to Jim.

I ramble on. "I've been working on some songs? I dunno if they're any good though. They're sort of different. I can't play like Matt yet, but..."

Fuck.

He takes his hat off. Puts it back on. Drains his hot-chocolate cup, but it's already empty, so he throws it at the garbage can. Misses. Swears. Goes to pick it up. Opens the trailer door and looks out. Yells at someone. I fucked up and talked about Matt. I'm not supposed to. But it's hard. When all Jim wants me to do is tell him about my life, and I don't have one. I always say something wrong, some kind of reminder. Because really, almost everything can be traced back to Matt.

I get sad, and Jim notices. That usually helps. If I get sadder than him. That tips the scales. "All right, come on, kiddo. We need some of your expertise upstairs."

"Yeah?"

"Grab that sledgehammer over there and follow me. Are those boots steel-toed?"

They're not, but close enough. I nod and follow him into the building, which has already been stripped and readied for demolition. He shows me how to check that the wall isn't load bearing, that there are no plumbing or electrical lines in the way, even though I know they've checked already. Jim only ever lets me smash nice clean walls.

"What do ya think, Champ?"

I appraise the wall, searching for the sweet spot. "Right there?" I point.

He nods. I swing. The sledgehammer lodges in the wall with a satisfying *thunk*, and when I yank it out the drywall splits right up the middle. I hit it again.

When we're done, the wall's been reduced to a pile of rubbish on the floor. I'm out of breath, and he looks pleased. "You're pretty good at that!"

I get an idea. "Do you think I could work for you sometimes?"

He blinks. "Like, doing demo?"

"Yeah. I'll do anything though. I could use the cash."

He's already reaching for his wallet and giving me forty bucks. "What do you need cash for? You should focus on your studies, Jo. You're so smart. You just buckle down and get into a good university. Maybe get some scholarships. You don't want to work with these chumps." He points out a couple of them and whispers, "They're all fresh out of Stony anyway."

This is the prison north of the city.

"It's one thing to come by and get some ya-yas out, but I don't want you working with these losers." A couple of these losers are near enough to hear him and look over. "What are you looking at? Get back to work! Can't you see we're having father-daughter time over here?" He presses the twenties into my hand. "Is that enough?" he asks. "You need bus fare? New clothes? How about a new guitar? I can take you to Long & McQuade after work. I've been meaning to take my bass in anyways. What do ya say?"

It's not the first time he's tried to take me to the music store and get me a new guitar. "It's okay, Dad. That's enough. Thank you."

Jim is Dad to his face and Jim behind his back. He's less vain and more sentimental than Maggie, who is always Maggie, never Mom. I don't have the heart to tell him I need four hundred bucks to pay off Maggie for my making phone calls he wouldn't have the heart to hear about. And I don't have the heart to tell him I need to amass a nest egg big enough to get me far away from this city and set me up somewhere that doesn't resemble here at all, not even a little bit. I don't have the heart for anything, so I just pick up the sledgehammer and knock down another wall.

~

The schedule for my movements between parental homes has unraveled. I go to Jim's when I can't stand Maggie. I go to Maggie's when I can't stand Jim. I'd ricochet more often between the two, but for Howl's sake I mostly stay at Maggie's. Howl is happier there, and in terms of creature comforts, so am I. Like I said, the basement is my refuge. I'd hide out down there reading and listening to records and practicing guitar all the time if it weren't for the wrath of Maggie, not to mention the risk of vitamin D deficiency and the fact there isn't a bathroom.

There's also the fact that my uncle Gord moved into Jim's place last summer when his wife left him. I think the idea was that they'd help each other out of their respective ruts, but from what I can see they've only gotten more comfortable. They live in the house Jim bought just south of the city after he and Maggie split when I was eight. Jim's place was new when he bought it, but that was a long time ago now, and in the last year especially it's gotten a bit gross—neither of them are big on housework, and Jim started fostering cats a while back. I used to try to clean up, but it's hard to know where to start. When you do start and you get something clean—say, you do all the dishes—then it just illuminates the mess everywhere else. So the trick is not to try.

We stop by the house when Jim's done for the day. He goes into his bedroom, and I hear the gurgle of his bong and then coughing. Two cats emerge from behind furniture and circle me curiously. I recognize the tabby, but there's a black one with white patches I've never seen. Gord stomps in the back door, slams it.

"Heya, Jo. How you been?" He sinks into the couch, puts his feet on the table, reaches without looking into the mini fridge, finds a beer and cracks it. Their interior designer must have been a teenage boy—the place is set up for the sole purpose of easy access to weed, beer and video games. I plunk down on the armchair, the only other available seating.

"Oh, you know." I shift a little in my seat, find a bowl wedged between some cushions and put it on the floor. The black cat sidles up to investigate. "Who's this?"

"That's Willie," he says. "And you remember Hank."

"I do."

"So," says Gord. "Got any of those swim meets coming up?"

"I quit the team, Uncle Gord. I don't swim anymore."

"Right," he says. "Good."

Jim returns red-eyed, relaxed. I'm supposed to pretend not to know he smokes pot.

"Long & McQuade and then Chinese? How's that sound?"

"Sure," I say, watching as he picks up his bass from a stand in the corner and packs it into a case. "What's wrong with your bass?"

"Nothing wrong really." He points at the table, which is so covered in junk it takes a minute for me to spot it—an orange flyer announcing that the Bootstraps are playing the Pyramid next month.

"You're playing a show?"

"Yeah," he says, swinging the bass case over his shoulder. "Fundraiser for Danny's sister. One of her kids is sick, and we're raising money so she can take time off work to be at the hospital."

"I thought the Bootstraps were retired."

"The Bootstraps retired?" Gord asks.

The Bootstraps is Jim's old band. They were locally famous before I was born. That's how he met Maggie. She would go to all their shows. By the time I came along, they were just playing a few times a year, wedding socials and fundraisers and fortieth-birthday parties. And then a while back they stopped completely.

"I changed my mind," he says, putting his jacket on. "Missed it. Besides, it's for a good cause. I've been meaning to take my bass in and get it set up. It's wonky from not being played for so long. Plus, we need to get you a new guitar. Something that screams *Jo!*"

The thought of anything screaming *Jo!* is disturbing, but I follow him out to the truck anyway.

⁓

Jim's buddy Zack works at Long & McQuade. He says he'll set the bass up while we wait. I'm ordered to look around and find a guitar. Really I want to watch to see what Zack is doing at his workbench, but Jim insists, so I just listen to them talk about fret wear and whammy bars and how bowed the neck of the bass is while I find the cheapest guitars and try them out.

Maggie always says never date a bass player. "Only twisted individuals play bass, Jolene," she'll tell me when she's had too much gin, the only time she ever talks about Jim. She's against guitarists too. "Egomaniacs—they just love ya and leave ya. What you want to do is get yourself a drummer. Drummers may not be smart, but you can depend on them."

I think I can depend on Jim, so long as I don't expect him to attend parent-teacher conferences or help me with my homework or model responsible adult behavior. Empty praise from one's stoner dad only goes so far, but it's nice to know there's someone I can't let down.

It occurs to me I could pick a guitar so expensive Jim can't afford to buy it for me, so I broaden my search.

"That one's a beaut," Zack calls across the store when I reach for a flashy red Stratocaster.

"Yeah, you look rock 'n' roll, sweetie," Jim says, and I blush. There are other people in here. Boys, of course. It's weird being a girl in one of these stores. I always feel like the dudes that shop and work here think I'm just waiting around for a guy. Which I guess I sort of am. I take the Strat over to the amp Zack set me up with and play the song I've been working on. Quietly, but I play it. I can hear Jim saying something about buzzing and action and other guitar talk I don't understand, and I see one of the long-haired dudes browsing the guitar mags look at me sideways, and I play on.

"So, is that the one?" Jim asks. I jump. He and Zack have come out from behind the counter and are beside me.

"It's a great, versatile guitar. You'll play it for years," Zack says.

It's also nine hundred dollars. "No, no," I say, lifting it over my head and handing it back to him. I try to change the subject. "Hey, can you show me how to lower the action?"

"Ring it through, Zack," Jim says, taking out his wallet.

"No, Dad, seriously. I don't want it."

"You deserve your own guitar," he says. I can see his resolve, but I can't make the argument that would work against it: that I have plenty of perfectly good guitars—he just doesn't want me to play them.

"I don't want a guitar. I want, uhh, that." We're standing beside a display case full of pedals, and I point at one with a price tag under a hundred dollars.

"The Boss loop pedal," says Zack. "You into looping?"

"I'm getting into it, yeah."

"That's pretty cool," says Jim. "Do you know how to use it?"

"Kind of. I'll learn."

"That's a good starter looping system," Zack says. I nod as if I know what that means. "Very intuitive. She'll figure it out in no time."

Jim nods. "Wrap it up then." The guitar goes back, and I breathe easier. A few minutes later Jim and I are back in the truck, headed for the Chinese restaurant. I get him talking about tress rods and other terms I heard him and Zack use, and he's off. I follow as best I can. I want to walk into those stores and feel like I belong there. I want to know I do.

⌣

"I got you a job." Maggie never comes down here. Just yells down the stairs. I am fooling around with the loop pedal but stop at the sound of her voice. She repeats herself a few more times. "I got you a job." And again. "I got you a job." She sounds plastered. Or maybe just pleased.

Against my better judgment I go upstairs. I find her in the kitchen. Char is at the table, her head swathed in plastic wrap.

Maggie dyes her hair for her once a month. Red this time. Fire engine, by the looks of it.

Maggie leans against the counter. "Winston at the Cal was looking for someone. Kitchen help. I signed you up. You start tomorrow."

"I'm not working at the Cal."

"Why not?"

"Look at it this way, Jo," Char says. "You'll get tipped out. Pay off that phone bill fast." Baby is attempting to claw her way up Char's front but can't scale her cleavage.

"It's not legal for minors to work in bars."

"Job's a job, Jo. Doesn't have to be legal."

"I think that's only if you're the one serving alcohol," Char says. "You'll just be washing dishes, right, Mags?"

"Yeah," Maggie says, smug. "You don't have to be eighteen to wash dishes."

"Plus you'll probably get paid under the table." Char tries again, distracted because Baby's claws have caught in her sweater and she can't get her off.

I go out. It's too cold for breathing, so I don't. Not until the river, where I scream. Silently. The snow is rough when I plunge my hands into it, a layer of crunchy ice on top. I grab two palms full and rub it across my face to cool down. To numb over. I don't want to be here, I don't want to be here, I don't want to be here, but I am.

Howl looks over from where she's sniffing the foot of a tree. She looks at me and says, *You can't go now. You've got to grow up first.*

But I don't have time for that.

Well then, says Howl, *maybe Maggie has a point. Work at the Cal. Make some money. Get on a bus out of town. How else are you going to leave? You can't walk out.*

But I do not want to admit she has a point right now. Howl knows. Howl slinks off through the trees to smell other smells and chase other shadows. Leaves me to stare angry at the moon.

~

Turns out the loop pedal lets you build a noise bigger than yourself. I don't need anyone else—I can record a beat and layer guitars over top and then add my voice, just by stepping on the pedal. It remembers what I tell it to do and forgets what I tell it to forget too, which is more than I can say for most people. Who needs a band? Who needs anyone? I can make all the noise I need on my own.

SEVEN

"So why do you need a job? You saving up for a car? Or a new cell phone? Or what?" Groves is reading over my paper on weather as theme in literature. I told her it was for an essay-writing contest, and she actually believed me. She's too focused on her other line of questioning.

"Lots of students have jobs. It's not weird."

"Just the way you said it. Like you have debts to settle or something."

"I'm saving up for after high school is over."

She nods. "That's great, Jolene. So what's your plan today?"

"I dunno."

"Good one," she says, and then, "You appear not to know how to use a semicolon."

"Yeah, I usually just stick one in when it feels right."

She looks scandalized. "Oh, that's not going to do. Let me get my grammar books."

I groan, but I also pull my chair closer and pay attention.

"And here I thought I was the one who was gonna be late. Come on, space cadet," Ivy says, surprising me a few hours later in my usual spot at the university, by the escalators. Before I can protest, she's strong-arming me down the hall. My muscles melted when I quit swimming, and I'm powerless.

"Nice to see you, ladies," the professor says as we grab a couple of seats near the back. "You're just in time to hand in your essays."

Ivy pulls hers out of her bag, smoothing the crumples out of it. She holds out her hand for mine. Cornered, I reach into my backpack. I don't know why I wrote it, but I did write it, then got Groves to help me edit it this morning. I watch my paper be passed from hand to hand to the front of the room and sink a little lower in my seat. I didn't put my name on it. Maybe some other student who is legitimately in this class but didn't do their homework will get the credit for it. I'm doing a good deed.

"I wanna show you something after class," Ivy whispers.

I nod. I'd thought if I lurked outside the doors until class started, then slipped in and sat at the back, I could avoid her, but no. Of course not. I should have just stayed at my actual school and attended my actual classes for actual credit, but I was too nervous about my first day at work later for that. And I wanted to see what the professor would assign next. I guess I wanted to see Ivy again too. I think.

HOW FAR WE GO AND HOW FAST

~

"Well, that was stupid and boring," Ivy says after class lets out. "Let's get coffee. I'm tired now."

"Um, sure." We walk down the hall to the cafeteria, and I don't have time to feel nervous—the questions come hard and fast.

"Where were you last class? You can borrow my notes if you want to. Professor Sinclair is pretty tough, don't you think? How's the guitar playing coming along? Can I hear some of your music sometime? Or are you shy about that stuff? What other classes are you taking?"

I stand in front of the coffee offerings, trying to choose between Colombian and French roasts while also coming up with a suitable lie. "Uh, a psych course and—"

"Do you have Reynolds? I had him last semester."

"Uh, yeah." I follow her to the lineup to pay. She gives the lady a five to cover both of us and shushes me when I protest.

"Come on. It's this way," she says, leading me to the escalators.

"Where are we going?"

She smiles. "Patience. I'm taking you to one of my favorite spots."

The escalator deposits us on the second floor, and Ivy keeps going up another escalator. "The library?" I ask as it comes into view. I've spent my fair share of time in there. If there are any good spots, I know about them.

"Sort of." The library is on the top two floors of the building. I follow Ivy across the lobby to the staircase that leads to the main stacks. She climbs the stairs quickly. I have to hurry to keep up, and then we're going down one aisle and then another, squeezing past students who are squatting in search of books or spread out on the floor with their research around them. Ivy stops in front of the door to a private study room. You have to reserve them at the main desk, but Ivy barges in. Two guys look up from their books in alarm. Engineering students, I'd wager. Pale, poor fashion sense, seem genuinely frightened of girls. "Shh," she says. "It's okay. We work here."

On the other side of their table is a door marked *Do not enter*. She starts to open it, and I freak. "Wait! It says *Alarm will sound*."

"It won't," she says. "Trust me."

"What's out there?" I ask, though I think I know.

Ivy leans close before she answers, eyeing the engineers. "The roof, duh. But be cool. I don't want a bunch of people to find out."

My stomach turns over. "But it's cold out."

"Oh, come on. It's pretty sheltered up there, not too windy. And the view is so cool. You can handle the cold for a few minutes. It's worth it."

I almost say yes. Almost continue following her where I'm not supposed to go. But my head begins to shake of its own accord. All of me does. "I can't. I've gotta go."

The engineers look up, irritated, as I run off like a moron. Even they are cooler than I am.

～

The Caledonia is king among scum hotels, six floors of basic cable, shitty carpeting and rooms that rent by the hour, perfect for all your crack-smoking needs. A dull fluorescent sign hangs from the side of the building, looking like it might fall off at any minute and land in front of the ground-floor beverage room, which hosts weekly amateur-stripper nights and other entertainments. Hang around for a while and you might be lucky enough to catch a curb stomping or a hooker with a bloody nose. It's a regular Winnipeg tourist attraction.

The scent of piss and beer greets me at the door. Also, a bouncer. He's bald and squat with a permanently creased forehead and shoulders as big and meaty as Easter hams. He's so jacked he has to hold his arms away from his body, like his muscles are shopping bags he can never set down. "ID?" he asks in a consoling tone.

Winston, the owner, spots me and comes out from behind the bar. "Jolene, you're looking all grown-up." He nods at the bouncer. "This is Maggie's girl."

Mr. Beefcake looks at me anew, probably searching for a likeness, which I fucking pray he can't find. He puts out a bloated palm, and we shake. His grip is surprisingly dainty, like he's used to being conscious to not crush things. "Your mom's going to kill it this week. We're all rooting for her."

There's a poster for the contest on the wall behind him. The prize is five hundred bucks and a trip to Vegas. No wonder she's so serious about this. Vegas is her spiritual homeland.

Winston leads me over to the bar. The room is low-key, just a few drinkers bent over tall glasses of beer and a row of gamblers at the slots with their backs to the room, oblivious to any and everything outside the rattle and clang of the machines. The slot zombies always make me sad. Self-destruction shouldn't be done out in the open like that. It's too much like watching someone slowly drown.

A waitress I've never seen before is behind the bar, stocking the beer fridge.

"Tina, this is Jolene. She'll be helping Benny out in the back on busy nights from now on."

Tina sticks out a hand, and I shake it. She's decorated with blue-black ink, the deliberate, childlike lines of homemade tattoos. There's a cross on her shoulder and a series of initials scattered across her chest, like she's had to add more and more letters to her skin, deviating from the plan, if there ever was one. She looks at me hard, appraisingly, and I force myself not to fidget. "You don't look like your mom," she says, and I love her.

"Basically," Winston says, "you can come in whenever Benny thinks he needs you. Busiest nights are Thursday through Saturday. Thursday's the contest this month, straight-up karaoke night the rest of the time. Friday is amateur strip night—that's big money. And Saturday rotates. Sometimes we get a cover band. Sometimes it's just dance music. Always got a meat draw though. People come out for that. Especially toward the end of the month."

I nod. Many a Sunday we have dined on Maggie's meat-draw winnings.

Winston leads me back to the kitchen, a space of yellowed tile and dull stainless steel. Benny's at the stove in his whites, which are more like grays.

"Jo!"

"Oof," I say as he hugs me somewhat violently. He smells greasy in a good way. "Hi, Benny." I wasn't sure he'd remember me. It's been years since we used to come around looking for Maggie, and I have one of those faces people forget. Or maybe it's not my face. Maybe it's something else.

"Welcome aboard," he says, waving one hand across the kitchen as if it's something glorious to behold.

"Thanks."

Winston claps his hands. "I'll leave you two to it."

"Thought he'd never go," Benny says after Winston leaves. "He only comes back here once every few months to complain about how much money we aren't making off the food menu. Meanwhile he's getting rich off the gambling revenue and serving people way too wasted to notice they're being charged double for their rye and Cokes. Not Tina though. She's a good one. But the other waitresses, they're cold-blooded. Anyway, this is Maude." He opens the dishwasher door, and steam pours out. "She's got some quirks. You're gonna want to get on her good side."

All day I'd been dreading this. But it's not so bad. It's almost easy. Benny may even be the perfect companion for me—he doesn't require my involvement to carry on a conversation. He just talks and talks, and I don't say anything.

Benny lets me go around eleven, when the kitchen closes. "I'll clean up myself tonight."

"Should I come same time tomorrow?"

"Nah, tomorrow's stripper night. Let's spare you that for now."

I hang up my apron and get out of there before he can start talking again.

"Hey, you're not walking, are you?" Tina asks as I pass by the bar.

"Nope," I say over my shoulder.

I walk by abandoned gas stations and corner stores and hair salons with hand-painted signs. I walk by the local Pay Day Loans, always a happening spot. The ground sails by beneath my feet, which seem divorced from my body, acting of their own accord. I walk so fast my footsteps blend together into one steady sound. I walk without a thought to traffic signs or rules of the road. I walk and walk until I reach the foot of the Salter Street Bridge, and then I stop.

EIGHT

Matt liked doing stupid, reckless things to prove to himself that he could. Ivy reminds me of him that way. He'd seek out risks, climbing trees no one else could scale, walking across the train yards at night instead of taking the bridge, riding his bike with no hands down the river path in the thick pitch-dark. Sometimes he would work for Jim and sneak on site at night, after the crew had gone home, and climb to the top of a doomed building to take in the view. And that was just the stuff he told me about. I'm sure there was more. I know there was.

The summer right after Matt got his license, we spent all our time driving around in the Illegal Mobile, Matt fussing with the tape player, me with my arm out the window to feel the air fly by.

A few sweltering days in a row had turned the house into a sweatbox, making the only tolerable activity—in between cold showers—taking turns sitting in front of our one fan. Matt mentioned a cliff-jumping spot that one of his co-workers at the pizza joint had told him about. We loaded up on chips and sodas and drove out. The car smelled of Maggie's perfume and the sunscreen we bought and applied in secret because of her near-religious belief that getting a sunburn builds immunities.

Matt parked next to a few other cars, and we followed the trail his buddy had described through a forest of poplars and pines and up to a cliff looking out on a lake that shone like polished silver in the full daylight. It was a local drinking spot, and a group of teenagers in bikinis and Bermuda shorts stood around at the edge. We dropped our towels and stripped down to our suits. Matt chatted up the only guy who was already wet while I looked over the edge and judged the fall to be about the same distance as the highest diving platform at the pool where I trained, which we'd sometimes get to jump off in the last minutes of practice. More important, I saw you didn't have to jump out very far to clear the cliff face. The guy told Matt the water was deep.

"Well," said Matt. "Shall we?"

"Let's," I said. He took three fast steps and was gone. The teenagers looked up from their drinking game to cheer him on. I was eleven, wearing my blue practice Speedo and already too tall. I was as frightened of teenagers then as I am now, and I knew dillydallying to be the enemy of daredevil activity, so when I saw Matt surface and swim over to the rocks, I filled my lungs with air and jumped.

The moment I hit the water and shot through it, I kicked like mad, surfacing in time to hear the impressed whoops of the teens up above. I swam over to Matt, whose skin had already dried in the searing heat. "Again?" he asked, reaching for my hand and hauling me out.

"Again," I agreed.

We jumped until our skin was pink and sore from being slapped around by the water. The teenagers treated me like a minor celebrity that day and every other time we drove out to the cliffs that summer. I didn't see how it was so impressive. Back then stuff like that didn't scare me. I knew it was easy, the same trick, really, as anytime you let yourself fall. The thing is, once you decide, it's already done. It's just a matter of committing. What people are afraid of is the moment after the decision is made, after you act but before you begin to fall.

Falling is easy. The moment before you fall is not.

If you break a second down into hundredths and then thousandths, that's how long this moment lasts. A sliver of a second, even then a unit of time I was more acquainted with than some. It's the difference between winning and losing, between hanging in the air and falling through it. It's an instant that stretches out longer than gravity should allow, long enough for you to panic, wish your feet were back on the ground. But I loved it, was addicted to that private fraction of a moment. It was like a secret I discovered and kept to myself, not telling the teenagers with their vodka coolers and their tans. I didn't even tell Matt, though maybe I should have.

Anyway, he was never so obviously proud of me as he was when I was throwing myself off that cliff, back when I was brave.

NINE

I stand at the foot of the bridge for a full five minutes. It feels like a full five anyway. But it's too late to go any other way. The streets around the tracks aren't good after dark.

Let's go, I tell my feet, spurring them forward, like a horse that's been spooked.

The Salter Street Bridge forms a great brontosaurus-like arch over the tracks, climbing so gradually its progress is almost elegant. The lights of the city are all around, a smattering of tall buildings downtown the only thing that interrupts the sprawl. On the tracks below, shadow trains pause in their passage from one side of the continent to the other. We're smack in the center of the country, the halfway point, the geographical middle of nowhere.

They say that thugs sometimes wait at the top of the bridge, where there's exactly nowhere to run. They'll jump you for your sneakers or your jacket, tear the headphones from your ears and the phone from your pocket. I don't have anything anyone would bother jumping me for. That's not why I worry about bridges.

At the top of the bridge the incline levels out for a moment, and I force my eyes up. A Viking comes toward me, but I know him—everyone does. You often see him walking around the North End. He looks like a normal workaday guy, except he wears this dollar-store Viking helmet that makes him nearly seven feet tall. We keep to our respective sides of the path as we pass, and when he's gone the bridge starts to slope down, and then I'm back on the ground and can breathe again. I let my feet carry me home.

Maggie is passed out on the couch, her head on Louie's shoulder. He's watching one of the celebrity news shows she likes. He raises one hand and nods at me silently, so he doesn't wake her. I want to tell him that if she's so drunk she's blacked out by midnight, she's not gonna wake easy, but I don't. I'm just glad she's not awake to interrogate me about my first day on the job.

The kitchen is clean, counters wiped down, leftovers from dinner stowed in Tupperware in the fridge. When did we acquire Tupperware? I let Howl into the backyard. *Sorry, girl. No walk tonight. Too tired. Blame Maggie. She's the one who got me a bar job.*

But Howl doesn't even seem to mind. I watch her circle the backyard once and then come wait by the door for me to let her in. I do, then head to the basement, pick up Shredder and plug in.

I play until I can't feel my fingers. Until I can't feel my toes. Until I can't feel a thing. Then I have to put the guitar down. Close my eyes and try to sleep.

~

I try and try to sleep.

I go underneath the covers, try singing silently.

When everyone is sleeping, the music in my head won't stop. It gets louder.

I get up again. Pick up the guitar again. Play my songs again. I'm getting better at looping. It wasn't hard to figure out. You just step on the pedal when you want to record, then build and build a creeping, haunting sound.

I wonder what Matt would think of my music. He listened to everything, but the blues were his first love, the root of what we played together. I don't know what to call these songs I've been writing. If they're rock 'n' roll or what. But I do know that when I play, it gets less loud in my head. Lets some of the noise out.

I could always go west, the way Matt went. He'd called when he got there. I picked up the phone and it was him. I'd been holding his leaving against him, but at the sound of his voice I forgave him all at once, in a rush. He was still gone, but there was his voice on the phone, telling me about the guy who smoked crack on the bus and got kicked off in Kamloops. About how he had to survive the two-day ride without any music once his iPod died and that it wasn't so bad, having an empty head. *I just sang silently*, he said. *What's the city like?* I asked and he said, *Hilly and green. More hills and more green than you can imagine*, he said. He said the mountains surrounded the city, hanging in the sky in a way that didn't look real. Like they were a hologram illusion, not something you could actually touch if you got close enough to try. He said he'd found a good record store and beaches you could walk along all day but that the word on the street was the music scene wasn't very accessible. People mostly went to clubs or hard-core punk shows. He said he would've tried sleeping on the beach, but it kept raining at night. A dude he met said he should try the island if he was just looking for a cheap place to bum around, bars to play music in most nights. Buddy gave him the name of a hostel, said his friend worked there, that if Matt dropped his name the guy would probably buy him a drink at the bar and tell him what he needed to know about the town to have a good time.

I'm catching a ferry tomorrow, Matt said. Then Maggie took the phone.

How could you take off on me like that? she yelled. But in a minute they were laughing. Maggie never got mad at Matt for long. She'd be mad for a moment, but then he'd unwind her, I don't know how. She complained to him for a few minutes about some injustice done to her by one of the other drunks in her friend group, and I stood there to be close to him, and then Matt's quarters had run out and he said he'd call when he got to the island, probably not the next day but in a day or two. And he did call, for a while.

So I could go west, except I'd stop in the city. I wouldn't go to the island, where he went, because islands are hard to leave by virtue of being islands, and once I start leaving I might never stop. I might get really good at it.

TEN

Louie has been here for five days straight. I'm pretty sure. Every time I leave and come back, he's here. She's got him good. He was scraping the black stuff out of the bottom of the oven last night. The pile of beer bottles by the back door is immaculate, and he's forever emptying ashtrays and bringing Maggie cups of tea. As if Maggie drinks tea. That's like feeding salad to a pit bull. She must be spiking it with something when he's not looking. Also, he cooks. First it was chili, then butternut-squash ravioli and now chicken soup because Maggie is feeling under the weather, which means hungover, but he doesn't know that yet. He brought the big pot in from the back porch, the one used to chill the beers at barbecues in the summer. It's huge, that pot, and Louie keeps using it to cook more food than we can eat. I've been filling Tupperware and old yogurt containers when no one is around and hiding them in the back of the freezer for later, once he's gone. It's going to be a long winter. We never eat this well.

~

It only takes a few shifts before I've made friends with Maude. The hose is called a snake, and it's suspended above the sink so you have to use your whole body to maneuver it. There's a piece at the end you squeeze to make it spray, and when you let go it bobs around. Sometimes it hits me in the face when I bend over to open up Maude's door. Tina intimidates me at first, but I tell a few of Cory's dirtiest jokes, look her in the eye when she teases me and then I'm in. More or less. She starts telling me stories about growing up on the rez and joins me out back for smoke breaks sometimes. I have a list of tasks, and I complete them. I scrub out the stockpots and scrape down the grill. I sweep, mop and manhandle unwieldy bags of garbage into the Dumpster out back. One night I get ambitious and pull out the range so I can clean behind it too. Big mistake. I witness all kinds of horrors. "I don't think anyone's ever done that before," Benny says, and I believe him.

After a few hours of work Benny makes me something to eat, kicks a milk crate my way and orders me to sit. Then he slips me a smoke, and I go into the alley without a coat on even, I'm so hot from the work. By the time I've sucked it down, the front of my apron is frozen, and I'm shivering and happy to get back to it. Benny tries to get me to go out and eat my staff meal at the bar, but I mostly manage not to. I like to pretend "out there" isn't happening. And that works pretty well.

I can tell karaoke night is busy because I don't have time to look up from the sink. I just aim my snake and blast food off plate after plate, obliterating ketchup and bits of chili, sending fries down the drain, loading up the racks as full as possible and closing Maude's door with a slight hip check, opening it again when the cycle is finished and getting a face full of steam.

"Hey." Tina appears in the doorway. She's not frazzled but in battle mode, no movement uncalculated. There are beers to be opened, plates to be delivered, drunks to be put in their place. The times when I'm forced to go out front, to restock the ice or bring out an order if it's busy, I do like that I get to watch Tina work. She pours drinks like it's dancing, or like it's chess and she sees three moves ahead. She's the law in this town, commanding respect with just the squaring of her shoulders and the cast of her eyes. "Maggie's about to sing," she says, like I'd want to know.

"Go on," says Benny. "The dish pile will wait."

"No." I shake my head and shake my head until Tina rolls her eyes and says, "Whatever," and Benny looks down like he's embarrassed. For me.

The rest of the night I don't look up from the sink even when it slows. I just aim the snake and blast crap off plates. I annihilate every mess. I make everything clean.

I get off work and push through the crowd, but not so fast that I don't hear the score. She's made it to the next round. There's big money on the line, not to mention Vegas.

George, the bouncer, stops me at the doors. "Winston wants to see you in his office."

I must look scared, because he pats me on the shoulder. "S'okay, sweetie. I don't think he's canning you yet."

Winston's office is down the hall that also contains the bathrooms. For this reason and maybe others, there's a bit of a smell. I knock, and he barks to come in.

"Hi…you wanted to see me?"

"What? Oh. Right." He rubs his jaw and sips from a mug I know from Tina contains whiskey. "Here—Benny says you're doing a good job. Keep it up."

I take the envelope he holds out and don't look inside despite the thickness of it. I put it in my pocket and go to wait for the bus that will take me on my roundabout journey home. After the first night I remembered to take the underpass on Main to get back to the North End, even though avoiding the bridge is a pain in the ass. When I'm sitting at the back of the nearly empty bus, I peek inside the envelope, and my stomach does a funny thing. It's like it soars and plummets at the same time. At home I hide the money under the mattress in the basement, sit down on top of it and think.

~

"So is this your office or something? I always find you here."

I look up from my notebook. I'm at my spot by the escalators, trying to come up with lyrics for a new song.

"I guess," I say, as Ivy plops down beside me on the bench and takes a bite of the sandwich she's holding in one hand. A piece of lettuce falls onto her lap.

"You skipped today too, huh?"

"Yeah."

She nods. The dye in her hair has almost faded out, leaving it a silvery gray. Or maybe she dyed it that way? I don't know how these things work. "I'm having a hard time making myself show up for class, man. I told you I'm going to art school next year, right? They're taking my transfer credits so I can't flunk out, but I'm not exactly invested. I just want to make cool art, ya know?"

"Yeah." She doesn't seem to think I'm insane, but I try not to say much just in case.

"Hey, what are you doing right now? Want to get high and go to the art gallery with me? Come on. It'll be fun. I'm meeting my friend there in a few minutes."

I do want to. But there are too many variables. Like, what'll we do once we're high at the art gallery? Who is this friend? What if he or she isn't as tolerant of my weirdness as Ivy seems to be? And how high exactly does she intend on getting? Then I remember I've got an actual real-life excuse for once. "Thanks, but I've gotta get to work soon."

"That sucks," she says. "Where do you work?"

"The Caledonia? Over on Isabel?"

"No way! That place is badass!"

It takes me a minute to realize she isn't making fun of me. "I guess?"

"I have to come visit you. I always wanted to go in there, but I was a little afraid of getting shanked. Do you think I'd get shanked in there? What night do you recommend going? I'm not into amateur strip night. That shit's depressing. Maybe karaoke night? I bet that's golden."

"No!"

Her face is surprised at first, but then it settles back into its usual amused expression. "No, not golden?"

"No, well, I guess it's golden, if you like watching sad drunks mangle music—"

"Oh," she says, "I really do."

"Well, it's kind of a rough scene. Have you ever heard of welfare Wednesday? See, karaoke night is on Thursdays, so like, the welfare checks have cleared by then, and everyone has cash to burn." This is total nonsense, but I can't stop. "Don't ever come on karaoke night. You'd definitely get shanked. Maybe I'll, like, let you know when would be good?"

"Sweet!" she says. Before I can get away she insists I give her my number, and I do, but then I'm too embarrassed to mention that it's a landline, that my mother has confiscated my cell phone because I made too many long-distance phone calls, which is why I'm working at the Cal in the first place, meaning it does not make me cool. Not at all. Not even a little bit. Still. I can't help but walk away feeling like I may not have totally flubbed the encounter. I may have actually acted like an almost-cool human being.

～

Ivy wasn't wrong to be worried about waltzing into the Cal. The regulars don't take kindly to tourists. Matt taught me about tourists back when he took me to the blues jams at various downtown hotel beverage rooms. We'd go on summer nights when I didn't have to get up to swim in the morning, and I'd sit on a stool nursing a Coke under the watch of the bartender while Matt went onstage and played.

During the breaks, when the musicians put down their guitars and picked up their beers, Matt told me not to go to places like that without him, and then he taught me how to act if I ever did. The most important thing, he said, was not to be a tourist. These were the young people who came downtown from the south end and the suburbs, strutting into places like the Woodbine and the Windsor and the Cal like doing so earned them some kind of badass badge of honor. Not to mention you could go into the off-sales with ten dollars and walk out with a king can, a pack of Player's and a glory story.

The regulars never treated Matt or me like tourists. We were there for the music, but it was more than that. Matt had a way with a room. He'd walk in and it'd turn toward him. Whether or not you wanted to, you'd turn too.

～

I'm feeling subtly optimistic, so I stop in to see Earl at the pawnshop. No new guitars on the wall, but I noodle around on an acoustic for a few before sidling up to the counter. Earl's wearing his Jets jersey, as always, and a funny visor with a translucent yellow bill that casts a jaundiced glow across his craggy face. "Any chance you've seen a—"

"Nope." He cuts me off before I get the question out. I take it in stride.

"Okay, but how far away would an Xbox, a bunch of authentic mid-'90s concert T-shirts and a vaporizer get me?"

"Don't waste my time," he says, but as I'm leaving he takes pity and tells me the Xbox would get me to Brandon. "You're gonna have to up the ante if you wanna make the Manitoba border though."

It's just about the most encouraging thing I've heard all day.

ELEVEN

Something strange is happening at home. Every day things get a bit shinier.

"Isn't he great?" Char asks.

"Sure." I shrug.

"Come on. Look at this place. It's never been this tidy."

"I guess."

"I wish I could find a nice guy. I just meet one fucker after another."

"Where'd she meet him anyway?" I ask.

Char looks at me for a while before answering. "I thought Maggie would have told you."

"Since when does Maggie tell me anything?"

"Come here, Baby." She pulls the dog onto her lap.

"I think I deserve to know where the stranger in my home came from."

"Louie isn't strange. He's been in the picture for a while."

I snort. "Yeah, a week is pretty good for her. You're right."

"Jo, they've been dating for a couple of months now."

She's looking at me strange again, so I stand up. "Don't mind me—I just live here."

I stomp down the basement stairs like a typical teenage idiot. At least it was only Char, and I know she'll act like it never happened. I plug in. Who needs friends when you have a loop pedal? I have a whole band with the turn of a dial and a tap of my foot. I shouldn't be able to hear the knocking, hear them call my name for dinner, but I do hear. Doesn't matter. There's a lock on the door, and I turned it.

~

I'm sure of it now. Maggie is playing some kind of trick on me. On all of us.

Generally speaking, every morning my mother wakes up a monster. She can't form words, so she communicates in groans and growls. She can't hold her head up—it lists onto her shoulder, or she holds it in her hands. In those first few minutes of morning I don't think she knows who she is or who I am or how she wound up in our cluttered-ass house in this flaming Dumpster of a neighborhood we call home.

That much, at least, I can relate to.

The process of making Maggie human takes an hour, maybe two. It all hinges on what sort of shape she's in when her alarm starts blaring and she drags herself out of bed and down the hall to stand for several minutes under painfully hot water before beginning to wash.

When she emerges from the bathroom she's not quite a functional human being, but then, functionality isn't chief among Maggie's talents. She's as pretty as she ever is, though, all washed and half-awake. Not yet spackled in product from head to toe. Bathrobe wrapped around her body and a towel holding back her hair. My mother has a misled beauty. It's there, but she does everything in her power to obscure it. She's not cute, but she'd be regal if she left well enough alone. Too bad she tends toward clothes that make her look like a drag queen on a budget—short flared skirts and shirts bedazzled in the chest region.

That's how it's always been, since the dawn of time. So you can understand my confusion when I walk into the kitchen in the morning and find Maggie at the stove, barefaced and barely herself, wearing an apron, making eggs.

"Morning, hon," she says. "Omelet?"

I'm trying to wrap my head around the apron and don't notice Louie. I jump when he waves hello with the knife he's using to chop peppers.

"Do you want cheese in yours?" he asks. His English is fine. Did I imagine the accent? Or maybe he was putting it on? Also, where are the drunks?

"Louie-baby, could you help me roll this?" Maggie asks, doing her little-girl giggle. That's a bit better I suppose.

"Come on, Howl," I say, slapping my thigh for her to come.

"Louie took her out already."

"Pardon?"

"Louie took her out. He's an early riser."

Louie is an early riser. What's next? Louie pays his child support on time?

"Hey!" says Maggie. "How's the job going? Benny says you're a great worker."

I don't buy this bullshit show. I grab my jacket and take off. Walk to school because I have the time and I'm too mad. Have I mentioned that every time I leave, I leave like it's the last time? I make sure my room is tidy, no unmentionables about, all my records safely in their sleeves. It's part of my practice.

———

"Fancy meeting you here," Groves says, and I jump for the second time today. I'm smoking by the Dumpsters, and she's just popped her head around.

"Hey," I say, stubbing the cigarette out against the wall and tucking it back in the pack for later. I can tell I'm in trouble, but I'm not sure what kind.

"Looks like you're done there. Come inside. I've got something I want to run past you."

I shrug.

"Let me rephrase that. As your teacher, I hereby order you to come inside and join me in my classroom. Come on now! Let's go!"

I follow her in, but I mutter things you shouldn't say to a teacher under my breath as I'm doing it.

"Sit," she says when we're in her classroom. "What's on your mind?"

I'm thinking about Maggie's men. The guys she'd bring around, all casual at first, both sides acting like nothing was going on. This is my friend Mike or Fred or John. No matter how nonchalant she was about it, the time spent poring over herself in the mirror was one way we would know. I'm sure the guys knew too, but everyone pretended not to. Why is it you're supposed to do that? Act like you aren't after what you actually are. Love or sex or whatever. Anyway, at first all the dudes made nice, going, *Hey kid, whatcha reading, what grade are you in, here's ten bucks to go to the Sev, go out and play for a while.* And then a couple of weeks later he'd be in deep. When Matt was around it was almost fun, having new dads all the time. We'd call them that to make them squirm, extract all the guilt money we could out of them and enjoy the days or weeks or months they'd buy in good moods for Maggie before it went sour. Falling in love starts to look debasing after a while. I think it did something to me, watching the pattern repeat. It might have made me immune.

I think these things, and I know Groves is waiting on my answer, but my mind's so full I can't. I have to say something, though, so I say, "Nothing," briefly raising my eyes from the paper clip I'm bending back and forth. Eye contact helps make people less afraid of you. Or more. Depends on the kind.

Groves starts talking, the kind of talk where I just have to nod my head and say yeah every once in a while. Yes, I will be good. Yes, I see the error of my ways. From now on

I'll be a different way. I nod and I smile, and the whole time I'm running it in my head. How the Louie thing will go. Just like they always do.

The first-period bell rings, and I get up. "I have bio."

"Hold on," she says. "I need a student to help me move some boxes at lunch. Do you have plans?"

This is thinly veiled. We both know I don't.

I shrug. "Not really."

"Good," she says. "Meet me in the parking lot?"

This is not the first time Groves has tried to take me to a secondary location. Never let them take you to a secondary location. That's what the murder experts say on the cop shows Maggie watches. Not that I think she's going to murder me. But it is one thing to hang out with a teacher at school, quite another to take it off school property.

I daydream through bio and sleep through math. I have gym before lunch, but I never go to that, so I go to the library to see if they have the book I need for the English course at the university. They do. I start in on it.

～

She insists on taking me to the Olive Garden after a brief stop at the public library, where we pick up four boxes of books left over from a recent charity book sale.

"You know," she says, "my dad died when I was thirteen."

I am turning a napkin into confetti, and it requires all my concentration.

"He had a heart condition. We had no idea. The worst thing was that we didn't have any warning. Endings shouldn't come out of nowhere like that. You should get a chance to brace yourself."

I look at her hard until she stops.

TWELVE

After school I walk home the long way. Fat flakes of snow are coming down in globs, clinging to my face and everything. It's the sort of snow that smooths out all the edges of our homes. It makes everything look like a picture book, like a winter-in-the-hood snow globe. The streets and yards aren't littered with cigarette butts and Slurpee cups, the rooftops aren't in need of repair, and no car windows are broken.

Maggie and Louie are already home. Maybe they never left. Who knows. They're in the basement, in Matt's room, my room, where no one ever goes but me. There's a cardboard box at the top of the stairs. She's probably rooting around for a costume for her next karaoke number. She's got all kinds of things down there. Old Halloween stuff and stripper gear and other family heirlooms.

I go to my upstairs bedroom instead and doze off. The math nap wasn't enough. I drift in and out as noises infil-trate my blanket hideout. Char relaying the tale of her latest Internet dating escapade. Baby's shrill little yap. Louie banging pots and pans. Maggie singing "*Fever in the morning, fever all through the night.*" The muffled people sounds are breaking my heart, but don't let that impress you. These days everything breaks my heart. The way the sun goes down at four in the afternoon, the way there's hardly any day and so much night. The way the old guy in front of me at the corner store counts out change for his Scratch & Win, quarter by quarter, nickel by dime. That fucking space heater in the basement and the way it lulls me with its warm whirl and then cuts out. The teamwork of the garbagemen and their truck working down our back lane, yelling *Go!* at every empty dumpster. These things catch me off guard and wind me. I don't think I'm breathing right these days. I forget to.

I stand by my statement. I don't want to hear Groves's sob story. Or anyone's. There's nothing alluring to me about comparing my pain to someone else's. If you've ever felt it on a regular basis, you'll know sometimes nothing feels worse than the concern of others. But she was right about one thing: the hardest part is when something ends and you're not expecting it.

I can hear the tacky plastic sound of the cheapo karaoke machine from here, but I throw back the blankets and go downstairs anyway. The living room lights are turned low, and the canned karaoke track plays, finger snaps and a smooth, climbing bass line as Maggie croons, "*You give me fever...*" In her hands, Peggy Lee is pure drag-queen camp. I look in just long enough to catch her treating the poor standing lamp like a stripper pole, red feather boa around her shoulders, and then continue on to the kitchen. I wonder what Earl would give me for the karaoke machine. It's technically mine, a gift from an old boyfriend of Maggie's, the one we called Married Bill. (And we did call him that, all the time, to his face. *Hey, Married Bill*, Matt would say when he'd join us for dinner. *Want more potatoes?*)

Louie has laid out a spread of taco fixings on the table. I fix myself a plate and make to slip back upstairs, since it looks like she's still working on her wardrobe—the basement door is still open, boxes still in the hall. The song ends to polite applause as I pass by the doorway.

"When did you get home?" she says into the microphone.

I shrug.

"There's a message for you on the machine."

I go back to the kitchen and press *Play* on the answering machine as I eat my tacos, expecting to hear Benny's voice giving me my shifts for the week and getting something else instead.

"Hey! This is Ivy, calling for Jolene. I'm going to this party later and was wondering if you might want to come. Scratch that, I'm begging you. I know it's last-minute, but please come. It's an art show thing at a gallery on Ross. I hate the art crowd, but my friend's band is playing, and I promised I'd go to his last three shows but didn't because I'm almost positive his band sucks, and I absolutely hate standing around doing the I'm-so-cool head bob and pretending to enjoy the music but not too much because of course that wouldn't be cool.

Seriously, these people are a drag. So, wanna come? We can stand at the back and make fun of everyone! Please? If you don't say yes I'll be forced to drink copious amounts of wine from a box, wind up making fun of someone's stupid statement haircut or their stupid statement art and eventually I'll be politely asked to leave by the self-important shmucks who organized the whole lame-ass fandango, and everyone will stand around watching me be ejected from the party while pretending not to watch me be ejected from the party. That's a true story, by the way. Seriously, Jolene, only you can save me from the pitying gaze of the Winnipeg art crowd, all fifteen of them. Call me."

Before the machine clicks off she leaves the name of the gallery and the address. I erase the message in hopes Maggie hasn't heard it the whole way through (it's not the underage drinking she'd disapprove of, but the fact that she wasn't invited along) and take my dinner back up to my room.

Howl's stare bores into my head. She thinks I need to get out more.

I'm not a party person, I tell her. *I prefer solitary pursuits.*

I eat, and when I'm done I pick up my book and try to read, but Howl keeps sighing and being all *sometimes it's important to do things we're afraid of.*

I can hear laughter downstairs and the sound of furniture being moved around. I push it out of my head.

Then I get a bad feeling. A very bad feeling.

"Hey, Jo! Come here for a sec," Char calls from the couch when I reach the front hall, but I ignore her, push aside the boxes and beat Howl to the bottom of the basement stairs.

All the posters have been taken down from the walls. Milk crates full of records are piled on top of the dresser, and there's a neat stack of cardboard boxes in the corner. I pull open drawers, one after the other, and they're empty. Only the guitars and amps haven't been touched. Maggie comes up behind me like she's bracing for a fight.

"You packed up his shit?" I say.

"Could you spare us the scene?" she snaps, but she can't look at me. I look at her instead. Maybe if I stare hard enough, I can make her head explode. I give it a try.

"That's right." She heaves a long-suffering sigh. "I'm such a bad fucking mother."

I don't say anything, and she still looks everywhere but at me. Maybe I did inherit her death stare.

"Go ahead and hate me. You spend too much time down here. It's not good for you. There's not enough light."

"Right," I say. "My issue is not enough daylight. I just need more vitamin D."

She goes upstairs, and I grab the mattress money and follow her, intending to shove it in her face and say, *Here you go—now I don't owe you anything*, but I can hear her in the kitchen, ranting to Louie already, and I need to be outside *right now*. I grab my jacket and go.

"Hey!" She comes into the hall and yells after me. "We need to talk about that phone bill. Who were you calling?"

I walk out, and the universe is right there above me. Not a cloud, not a building overhead.

"Who were you calling, Jolene??"

I pull my hood up. There's no wind, but it's these still, clear nights that are the real cold ones.

THIRTEEN

The door girl takes my five bucks and marks the inside of my wrist with a Sharpie. She wears her hair all in her eyes, like she's so cool she doesn't need to see where she's going. I'd like to take notes on how she pulls this off, but Ivy is saying my name.

"Jolene! You came!" She goes for the hug. I don't hug easily, but I manage to submit to it without doing anything too alienating. "The band's about to go on," she says as we enter the room. "We're gonna have to elbow our way to the front."

The gallery has high tin ceilings that amplify the music pounding out of the speakers not far from where we stand. I'm not going to get away with mumbling tonight. I yell okay and she shouts that she'll be back in two shakes and then she's gone, fighting her way over to the folding-table bar, where a tall fellow who seems to be going for a Jesus look immediately engages her in conversation. Tonight her pastel hair is swept up in a bird's-nest knot at the back of her head like some kind of haphazard confection. She's wearing jeans and a denim jacket lined with thick fake fur. Denim on denim, and it works. ›

I shift from one foot to the other. I try to rearrange my face to mask my discomfort, but in the end I give up and walk over to the wall, which is hung with oversized photographs of sad cityscapes. No one else seems to be here to consider the art, but I circle the room, recognizing buildings, graffitied train cars and boarded-up storefronts. I study each photo in turn, and when I'm done Ivy still isn't back, and I can't see her anywhere.

At a bit of a distance and to an untrained eye, these people could be homeless, with their anti-hairstyles and laundry-hamper-looking clothes. They don't appear to be paying attention to me, but I feel observed anyway. I could just leave. The door is right there. But I stormed out of the house not an hour ago, and the thing about storms is, no one remembers the ones that just blow over. They have to rage on for a while.

"There you are!" Ivy appears and puts a beer in my hand. "Shall we do this thing?" She starts toward the stage without waiting for an answer. "I'm sorry in advance if this offends your sensibilities," she calls over her shoulder. "I haven't heard Drew's music in a while. It could be bad."

In front of me Ivy slips through the crowd, squeezing her slight frame in between the bodies of people talking in twos and threes. I struggle to fit myself through the gaps she's leaving in her wake. It turns out there's no stage, just a red-and-gold Persian rug on which the boys in the band are organizing themselves. A rough semicircle has formed around them, leaving space in front that suggests a dance floor.

Of course, that's where Ivy takes me, into the hole in the crowd at the feet of the band, where I am taller than everyone. I can feel their resentment burning at the back of my head as the house music cuts out and the drummer counts off.

They launch into it, and immediately the music is so arresting I forget to worry about how I'm obstructing sightlines. The band is a two-piece, the drummer and another guy on guitar, who hovers over a table spread with panels of dials and knobs I don't understand. Tattooed and spry, he hangs back from the microphone while his hands move between his guitar and these other strange instruments. I recognize a loop pedal under the table, which he steps on at intervals, building layers of spooky guitar sound and then tweaking them with a turn of a dial or by bending a string. When he opens his mouth, it's an ugly-beautiful thing. His voice is filtered through so many effects that I can't make out any words and don't need to.

The drummer plays with a messy intricacy, with all kinds of abandon. The kit looks makeshift—a kick drum, a snare and a cymbal. He has the sort of thick, floppy hair girls like to touch and then declare themselves jealous of, and, unlike his comrade, he appears to be uninked. I watch him watch the lead guy, waiting for the changes. The sound is quiet but large, and it stills the room, commands it, makes me want to

give up making music because I could never play like this and
go home and write a song.

Ivy is trying to talk to me, but she's so much shorter than
I am that I have to do a sort of half-squat maneuver to get low
enough for my ear to be anywhere near her mouth.

"What do you think?"

"They're interesting."

"Maybe a little too interesting?" She laughs, but I could
stand here studying them forever.

Abruptly it gets loud. The crowd swells behind me, and I
go flying forward. Ivy catches my arm and steadies me, but it
comes again, and I dig my heels into the ground to keep from
crashing into the band. The crowd isn't just close—it's closing
in. I'm sandwiched between bodies on all sides, bodies that
are jumping and shoving violently, like they've been waiting
all night for the cue to go apeshit and the band's just given it.

The bottle of beer, barely drunk, is ripped out of my hand.
My hat is yanked off and tossed into the air. I try to escape,
but it's impossible to do anything because staying on my feet
and not getting flattened now requires all my attention. I feel
hands on my back and a hard shove, and anger flares in me.
I ram a shoulder into the nearest chest, but there's no way
to tell if I nailed the asshole because everyone is pummeling
everyone else indifferently.

That's when it hits me. It's not personal. In fact, I think
it's impersonal.

I stop resisting the push and the shove, and in seconds I'm
bashing into bodies with the best of them. Beer sprays into

the air and lands on me like cool carbonated rain. Sweat drips down and soon I'm soaked, but so is everyone. My foot finds the fallen beer bottle. I lose my grip on the floor and go down, but right away strong hands grab me underneath the arms and yank me back up. I know without needing to be told that there's a code to this, an expectation that if you're knocked down, someone will pick you up again. A moment later a girl falls to her knees in front of me and I don't hesitate, hauling her up and shoving her back into the roiling mob.

In between jumps I catch flashes of Ivy. She's standing on a speaker, looking out. Then she's turning around and launching herself backward out over the crowd. Hands reach up and hold her, and she's passed around over our heads. As she floats my way, she starts sinking fast. I try to get close enough to catch her but only manage to put my face in the path of her falling shoulder. Tears flood the eye that took the hit, but I can't wipe them away because Ivy gets up, grabs my arms, and we jump up and down more savagely than before. They try to tear us apart, but Ivy's hold on me is tight. Hair sticks to my face, but I don't brush it away. My calves clench and cramp, but I carry on. I take an elbow to the head and feel my brain bang into the side of my skull, but still we jump.

The crowd is an organism unto itself, and I couldn't leave it now if I tried. And why would I want to? So I can go stand by the wall? I don't want walls tonight. Tonight I'm in the thick of it. I let a smile unfurl on my face, close my eyes, and throw my weight around.

⌒

"Thanks," the front man mumbles into the microphone before lifting his guitar over his head. In the audience we fall still, look around, dazed, like we can't remember what we were doing before we lost our collective shit. The last strands of feedback die out, and there's some applause, but it seems beside the point. Hip-hop comes over the sound system and chatter rises. People move toward the bar. I've lost Ivy but spot her in the lineup for drinks. I wander around looking for my hat. My legs are shaky and I move slow, letting the sweat dry on my skin. I'm not alone—around me there are others picking up shoes and items of clothing that were wrenched off them in battle.

I find my hat as Ivy comes back, all aglow. She hands me another beer. "I wasn't expecting that," she says. "These gallery shows are usually so tame."

"That was amazing," I say.

"You liked it? I wasn't sure. Mosh pits are an acquired taste."

"So that was a mosh pit?"

"Don't tell me you've never been in a mosh pit before!" She shoves my shoulder in disbelief. "Jesus, Jolene. What have you been doing with your life?"

I shrug. "Wasting it?"

"Well," she says, "not on my watch." She starts toward the door. "Always leave the party while you're still having fun. That's a rule of mine."

"What about our drinks?" I ask as she tilts her head back and drains hers.

"Bring it," she says, and I follow her out onto the street, pulling my hat on even though it's soggy from the mosh pit. Without a word we begin to run, hurtling away from the party, racing each other for old times' sake. Beer foam overflows the bottle in my hand, so I throw it at a wall, where it shatters. We laugh so much it hurts.

~

"Where are we going?" I huff a few minutes later when we slow to a giddy walk on a deserted street near the river.

"Remember I said I'd show you my art?"

"Yeah."

"Well, that's some up there." She points, and I look up at the sky. The stars are dizzying. She laughs. "No. Over there."

I follow her gaze to the building next to us. Painted on the wall about twenty feet up, a sharp-beaked bird is frozen in midflight, its wings blurred around their edges to suggest a weightless hovering.

"Oh," I say.

"I was into hummingbirds for a while," she says, unable to conceal her pride. "I'm on to peacocks now. Still working on getting the lines right."

I've got my head craned back to take it in. "How did you get up there?"

"Easy," she says, pointing to a series of rusted ladders that climbs the side of the building, which looks to be abandoned. "It's just a hop, skip and a jump up to the fire escape.

Then it's just your basic don't-look-down situation. The long swimmer's reach comes in handy." She hooks her thumbs through the straps of her backpack and motions down the street. "Come on. I've got something in mind."

She produces a can of beer from her bag, and we pass it back and forth as we walk. The only sound apart from what we're making is the ice on the river breaking up a block over, creaking like footsteps on old floorboards. We cross the street and go down another alley, where Ivy slows in front of a building. This one is definitely abandoned—the windows are bombed out, and scattershot graffiti decorates the exterior. We walk up to where the metal rungs of a ladder end in midair a few feet above our heads. Ivy hands me the beer, slips off her backpack and takes out a can of spray paint. She gives it a shake. "You coming?"

I stand in panicked silence, but Ivy doesn't press, just asks, "Can you whistle?"

"What?"

She pats me on the arm. "Just keep an eye out, hey?"

I still don't understand as she scrambles on top of the Dumpster and reaches for the lowest ladder rung, grabs hold and pulls herself up easily. Her muscles haven't melted like mine. I watch her climbing up and up, but then my stomach pitches to the left and the rest of my organs go right, and I have to put out a hand to keep from falling. Luckily, the wall's right there. I hold on to the brick of it and count sounds to calm myself. Ivy's feet on the metal ladder, then the hiss of spray paint. A heart beating, mine maybe.

The river groans, mutters to itself. I open my eyes but keep my hand on the wall. The nausea has gone, and a fury fills me instead. The mosh pit was one thing, but this is another. This is not what I signed up for. Not at all. Not even a little bit. I'm still fuming when I realize two dark figures have rounded the corner and are coming down the alley toward us.

I try to whistle, but nothing comes out. *Shit.* I try again and this time it works. A clear note leaves my lips and cuts through the night. Above me the hissing stops as two men step out of the shadows and into the glow of a streetlight. It's the boys from the band. "Hey, Ivy," calls the guitarist. "What's up?"

She leans out, looks down. "Drew? That you?"

They come to a halt in front of me, their arms full of gear. Drew is looking up, but the drummer watches me emerge from behind the Dumpster, where I've been cowering.

"Hi," he says, amused.

"Hey," I mumble as Ivy drops to the ground beside me. Together we back away and look up. A white bird floats on the wall two stories up where there wasn't one before.

"Swan?" asks Drew.

"Albino peacock," says Ivy. "I saw one at the zoo." She elbows me—too hard. "Pretty cool, huh?"

"Uh-huh," I say, and try to tell her with my eyes that I want to go. But she's in no rush.

"Jo, this is Drew and Graham. Drew and Graham, this is Jo. You guys need a hand?"

And then we're continuing down the alley, around the corner and up the street to their rehearsal space, where Drew fumbles for his keys before letting us in. Graham holds the door so I can go in first, and in the elevator he stares at me, and not in the way guys stare when they think you're pretty but in the way they stare when they think you're going to drop their expensive musical shit and break it. I hoist the amp a little higher in my arms. Maybe my muscles haven't completely melted yet. The elevator is too well lit and the walls are mirrors, and there's nowhere to look that doesn't make me more uncomfortable than I already am—and I am, and how. Ivy is explaining how we met, making it more than it actually was. Making me more than I actually am. I have to learn how to do that.

"Jo and I used to be rivals in another life. She's also in a band."

I shake my head. "I'm not in a band."

"So you're a singer-songwriter then?" Graham says, and it's clear that's an insult.

Douche, I think, but out loud I just say, "Gross" and feel a pang of relief when everyone laughs.

The doors slide open and we go down a long hall to another door, where Drew can't find the key but then does, and inside I put the amp down as super-extra gingerly as I can. When I straighten up, Graham's watching again, but I'm relieved, because now we can leave. Except no. Drew is grabbing beers from a little fridge, and Ivy is saying, "Of course we want to drink on the roof—are you kidding?" And then we're back in the elevator, going up to the roof. I hold my beer too tightly and the can crackles, and I keep opening my mouth to say I don't do rooftops and no I'm not kidding, but every time I open it nothing comes out, so I take a drink of beer instead. By the time the elevator doors open, the can is empty.

We're not there yet though. Now it's into the stairwell and up a flight to a maintenance room where pulleys and other elevator entrails hang out in the dark. In one corner a wooden ladder leads up to a trapdoor in the ceiling.

Ivy goes first, pushing the door open and disappearing out onto the roof. Drew follows and then Graham. I hang back, looking up at the square of empty sky. There's no way I can't, and there's no way I can. Graham's face appears in the opening. "You coming?"

I would give anything to be cool right now and follow him up that ladder, douche or no douche, but my head shakes of its own accord because my body doesn't listen to anything I tell it anymore. I'm headed for the exit when there's a thud behind me. "That's cool. I'll stay down here with you."

I turn around, and he's settled on the floor near the base of the ladder. He nods at the space beside him and I sit, careful I'm not too close, not too far away.

"My mom is super afraid of heights too," he says, and I feel blessed that it could be that easy. I'm afraid of heights. That's all.

"Hey!" Ivy peers down through the hole in the ceiling. "Come on, you guys! The view up here is crazy."

"Jo and I are going to hang down here," he says.

"Oh," says Ivy. She looks at me, an eyebrow raised, and I look away. I look at Graham. He hands me his beer, and I drink it. Usually people only call me Jo when they know me. But he doesn't know me, not at all. Not even a little bit. And suddenly that's appealing.

He's pulled out a joint and put it between his lips. He flicks a lighter alive and holds the flame to it until it's burning. While I watch him inhale I plan out how I'll decline when and if he offers, but then he holds it out and my hand reaches for it. Bad hand, I think, as the joint transfers between our fingers expertly. I put it between my lips, breathe in, and then I am warm when I didn't even realize I was cold. Relaxed when I didn't realize I was holding all kinds of parts of me tightly. "So what do you do?" he asks.

"I walk a lot," I say, breathing out smoke, and through the smoke I know I've said something strange, but I'm feeling beer brave, I'm feeling weed wise, and I don't care. I don't know if I've ever not cared this much in my life.

"You don't drive either?" he says, and I shake my head. "It's a fucked-up place to live without a car."

"I don't like cars."

"Same." He smiles and passes the joint back to me, and again I plan on declining and again I accept it instead.

"The thing about them is they go so far so fast. Too far and too fast. You can't take things in."

He nods. "I like to move more slowly," he says, stretching his legs out languidly in front of him. They are long, and thinner than mine by far. He looks up through the trapdoor to the sky and I follow.

"But you're a drummer," I say. "You're like, speedy and..." I lose what I was trying to say, cast around for the right words. "Like, always in motion."

"But I'm also staying still. Think about it—I move, but I don't go anywhere." He smiles. "Anyway, I try not to be one of those drummers that's always tapping things and keeping time," he says and demonstrates, beating his knee, the ground, my arm.

I find that curious. Not his hand on my arm. Well, that, but the other thing too. "Do you though? Keep time?"

"Yeah, I do. I hope I do. I try to keep it to myself though. Does that make sense?"

"It does," I say, and he looks at me, and just like that, I feel too far gone. Too in deep. I sit on my hands to keep them from doing anything else I haven't sanctioned, and Ivy's head appears in the trapdoor again.

"You kids behaving?" she says, and when we assure her we are, she disappears, and then Graham asks me what I listen to. Here is something I know—when talking to boys about music, prepare to be talked at. But it's not like that now. I don't know why I can talk to him, but I can. I do. I wonder if I could learn to keep time too.

FOURTEEN

Pavement streams by beneath my feet. There's nothing I love more than this, motoring along with my head full of music, the beat of my boots on the ground the only sound that infiltrates the private world I've encased myself in. At first I take Main, but I hang a left on Selkirk when I spot thuggish outlines up ahead. At Salter I cut north again. That's when I see him, coming toward me on the far side of the street. The Viking. I swear it's not the beers talking. It really is him—there's no mistaking that silhouette. He's walking alone, his full-length parka flapping open in the wind, the horned helmet perched as ever atop his head.

I smile at him, though I doubt he can see me, seeing as I'm a shadow in the night. Jolene, queen of the prairie sky.

I'm not sure exactly when I notice I can't walk in a straight line, but it's true. My legs seem determined to zig and zag down the sidewalk. And then I'm home! I must have made amazing time. I should always be drunk when I travel on foot.

I only realize after the fact that I've slammed the door behind me and am making way too much noise as I try to kick my boots off. When I bend down to loosen the laces, the room spins, and I reach for the wall, but whoa, is it ever not where I expect it to be.

No one is passed out on the floor or the couch or sitting half-awake, tipped forward at the kitchen table, and the basement is even more empty than last time I checked. I pick up the guitar and sit down on the unmade bed. There are faint rectangular outlines on the walls where the posters were.

I play the song that arrived in my head on the walk home. My fingers aren't as drunk as my feet, and they know all the right moves. It sounds like it might fall apart at any moment and almost does but never quite completely. I almost wish someone were around to hear how well I can play right now. I've never wanted that before.

FIFTEEN

In the morning Maggie wakes me up. I am lying on the bare
mattress in the basement. She hands me a piece of mail and
leaves. We do not speak, and I like it that way.

I stare at the envelope for a long time. I curl up around
it, staring. Something settles over my chest and puts down
roots. I try to get up, try to shake it off, but this thing won't
let me.

Maggie's left the door open, and Howl slips down the
stairs, puts her nose in my face.

Open it, she says.

I don't want to.

But why?

Because I don't want to.

We go back and forth about it for a while before I roll over
and test myself on a vertical plane. I stuff the envelope underneath the mattress, because whatever's inside it, now is not
the time, and I hobble upstairs. Mercifully, no one seems to be

home. I wash my face and brush my hair, then dig through my hamper, smelling T-shirts. No luck—they all stink like work. I consider borrowing something from Maggie's closet, but I'm not really the type to wear clothing that involves rhinestones. Instead I go back to the basement and root around in Matt's stuff until I find a box of clothes and pull out a suitable T-shirt. I smell it too, but there's nothing of him left on it.

The coffee maker sighs, watery, and I remember last night. With a fresh morning mind, I'm burning with embarrassment for every dumb thing I said. Other people have the privilege of drinking their faces off and forgetting all the stupid shit they get up to, but not me, oh no. I can hear myself asking Drew who he thought would win in a fight, James Brown or Joey Ramone. The Boss or the King? I remember getting angry, inexplicably, when Graham said he doesn't really get the blues and then writing down a list of artists and telling him to do his homework. Not to mention letting Ivy dance me around like we were stupid little good-time girls.

Oh jeez, the mosh pit. I even wish I could take back the mosh pit. Okay, so maybe that was kind of fun, but my leg muscles have been destroyed, and I probably looked terrible and sweaty, and who do I even think I am, carrying on like that? Maggie? I should know better. I'm supposed to be different. I'm not supposed to be like them.

Howl looks pissed.

This is your fault, I tell her. *I told you I'm not a party person.*

Eventually I manage to suit up to take Howl for a walk. Anything to get her to stop glaring at me.

The moment we step onto the porch, I can feel the difference. Something's shifted. Overnight the air's gone mild, like a switch flipped and all the bite drained right out of it. Newly enthusiastic, Howl launches off the steps and pulls me down the street. By the time we reach the river I'm sweating underneath my clothes. I unwind my scarf, pull off my hat. Branches droop under the weight of melting snow, which lands like heavy rain on my head.

It's freak spring.

It's a fake-out we fall for year after year. Freak spring appears one day in midwinter, months before you can reasonably expect the season to end. Temperatures climb ten, sometimes twenty, degrees in the night. Euphoria sweeps through town as everyone climbs down off whatever ledge winter forced them onto, and people go collectively apeshit, making out on park benches and lying around backyards in an effort to ditch the winter pallor, although the ground is soggy brown and the smell of melting dog shit dominates. Only a prairie person would try to get a tan when there's still snow on the ground. Being slightly in denial about your surroundings is the Winnipeg condition.

When it snows again—and it always snows again—everyone gets riled up, like the weather has been stringing us along. People are so stupid. They always expect good things to last. I try to be smarter than that. There's something about freak spring that feels, well, fake. The way it fools us into thinking it can wash us clean. Cleaner than we are. Cleaner than we should be.

I guess I'm only human, though, because after I've dragged Howl home and ditched the scarf, hat, mittens and extra socks, I walk back out into the gentle air feeling agile and free. I can't help myself. This is what I miss in winter. The privilege of being able to walk outside with your defenses down, without bracing yourself first. You can just walk out.

Today is not a day to go to school.

An empty king can of Coors rolls by, the Winnipeg equivalent of a tumbleweed. It's so eerily balmy out that even the bums outside the Windsor Hotel seem jolly and carefree. All along Main people are out in droves, drinking on stoops, calling out to each other, letting their bare limbs breathe. I catch myself smiling and force it off my face. I wouldn't want anyone to think I'm joining the freak-spring party, but a block later the smile creeps back into place.

As I make my way downtown I'm stopped by various street-side entrepreneurs and offered crack, weed, a yellow plastic flower, a deal on tube socks that fell off the back of the truck, and three rides anywhere I want to go. I politely decline them all. I catch a fistfight in front of the Woodbine and stop in at Earl's. He's reading an old *National Geographic*. I stand over the case of watches and wait for him to realize it's going to be one of those days. Eventually he sighs. "What?"

"I was just wondering…"

"What now?"

"How far away would a TV get me?"

"What kind?"

"I dunno. An old one."

"You'd be lucky to get to Brandon." He flips a page.

"What if I throw in a clock radio?"

"Still Brandon."

"A toaster oven?"

"Bran-don," he says it slowly, so I catch his drift.

"How about a TV, clock radio, toaster oven *and* a DVD player?"

"Saskatoon, maybe. If you caught me in a good mood."

"Okay."

"I don't have many good moods," he warns while I'm on my way out. Very few things in life reassure me the way Earl's detailed knowledge of Greyhound's ticket pricing does.

Despite my vow not to give in to the temptations of freak spring, I decide to take myself out for ice cream. Well, I don't decide so much as I realize I'm starving, and the nearest food establishment is an ice-cream place. I take it for a sign and go in.

I stand at the counter and wait for the employee to look up from his phone. He's a short guy with Buddy Holly glasses and greasy hair pulled back into the sort of man-ponytail Jim would call a dink knob. "You decide?" he asks after a minute.

"Can I get a scoop of that?" I ask, pointing into the freezer at something that looks like chocolate.

"Chocolate praline swirl? Or the Skor brownie?"

"The Skor one."

"Cup or cone?"

"Cup, please."

He rings me through indifferently, but as he's handing over my change he stops and squints at me from behind his thick black frames. "Hey, I know you."

"I don't think so."

"Yeah, I do! You went to Crescentwood, right?"

I grab my ice cream and put my wallet away. My stomach feels funny. I haven't eaten in too long. I need to get out of here. It's almost time to get to work. "No. I must have one of those faces. You know, like, a common face," I say moronically.

"I know!" He smacks the counter with his palm. "You're Matt Tucker's little sister, right? I'm Pete. I used to jam in your basement."

"Oh yeah." I bump into a table and put out my hand to steady it, or maybe to steady myself.

"How is Matty? I haven't seen him since high school. I heard he went out west."

"Yeah, he did."

"So what's he up to? He still out there?"

"I have to catch a bus."

"Hey! Next time Matt's in town, tell him to call me up! I'm putting together a band. We're gonna be called the Halfwits. Pretty good, huh?"

I run out of the store, trying to look sorry, which I am. That hasn't happened in a while. I add the ice-cream parlor to the list of places I don't go.

~

As long as I'm walking, I feel all right. It's staying still that's the problem.

SIXTEEN

"How's it going, kid?" Tina says as I throw myself at the bar.

"Coffee," I say. "Please."

She puts a mug in front of me and pours. "Whatsa matter?"

"Nothing." I tear a sugar packet open and dump it in. "Just tired."

"Huh," she says. "Because you look a tad hungover to me."

"Nope." I grab my coffee and head back to the kitchen. But maybe she's right. I do a body scan. I've never been hungover before. Maybe that's what's wrong with me today. Not the letter. Not freak-spring fever. And not ice-cream-parlor Pete. I've just got an old-fashioned hangover, like my mother before me.

~

My head is deep in a stockpot, where I'm using a large metal spoon as a chisel to scrape the burned stuff off the bottom.

Outside the pot Benny is saying how tomato sauce is the worst to clean.

"Wouldn't be so bad, but the lunch cook always burns the pots," I say.

"Yeah," Benny says. "He's a prick."

"Hey, Jo."

I come up for air and bump into the snake, which bobs up and down, dripping. It's Tina, looking pleased with herself. "Someone out here asking for you."

"I'm busy."

"No," she says. "I don't think you're too busy for this."

She sounds funny, so I assume it's Maggie out there, making some kind of a scene.

Benny gives me a nod. "Go on. It's time for your break anyways."

I hook the snake back in its holster and wipe my hands on my apron. "No way," Tina says, pointing at my front. "Take that off. And wipe your face—you've got some sauce on it. God, girl, just come here." She rubs some paper towel roughly across my chin, then uses it to dab the sweat off my forehead.

"It's the steam. It gets hot back here." I try not to wince as she smooths the frizz out of my hair.

"Come on." She shoves me forward. "Someone might've jumped him by now."

"Jumped who?" I ask as we walk through the kitchen doors, and I see Graham at the bar, punching at his phone with his thumbs. The wind has whipped his cheeks a bright, girlish pink, and he's dressed all in black—black jeans, black jacket and a black hat that he takes off when he sees me, touching his hand to his shaggy hair for a moment, as if he wants to rearrange it but then thinks better of it.

"Oh," I say. "I thought you were someone else."

It's not even a half smile he gives me, more like a quarter of one, but just like that, I get the sense I'm in grave danger again. "Who?" he asks.

"No one." I stiffen. Not my mother, that's for sure.

He says, "Cool," and he says, "What's up?" and if I wasn't totally inept at reading the facial expressions of anyone other than Howl, I'd say he's nervous too. But I am. So he couldn't be.

I say, "Not much," and I say, "Oh, you know, just washing dishes and shit." I gesture at my apron and then realize I'm not wearing it, so really all I've done is draw attention to my stomach area.

"Cool," he says, nodding excessively.

"What's up with you?"

"Not much. Drew and I just went to grab the rest of our gear from the gallery. Ivy mentioned last night that you work here. We were just a few blocks away, so I thought I'd check it out."

With the bar between us, I don't know what to do, so I grab a pitcher and fill it with beer. It's mostly foam, but I take two glasses and join him on the other side anyway.

"Oh." I pour him a glass and place it in front of him. "Well, I wouldn't come here alone. It's a bit shifty."

"What do you mean?" he asks. "I'm alone right now."

"No," I say. "I mean, don't come here when I'm not around."

He looks at me sidelong and says he wasn't planning to, and I feel stupid in a good way. I gulp my beer and say, "So." But what to follow it up with? "Umm, what are you taking at school?" I ask, immediately feeling like a mom—not mine but somebody's. "Sorry, that's a dumb question."

"Kind of like *what kind of music do you play?*" He takes a sip of beer while I burn with the sudden memory of reaming him out for asking me that last night. I believe I said that talking about genres of music grosses me out. "Philosophy," he says kindly. "I went to college for sound engineering already, but I decided to go back to school. I'll be the only sound engineer/philosopher around."

"Wow."

"What?"

"You've really gotta admire someone that unemployable." It just slips out before I can stop it.

He laughs and I do too, and we both sip, and I'm feeling pretty good. I'm feeling kind of awesome actually.

"What's yours?" he asks.

"My what?"

"Your major."

"Oh, yeah." The thing about the beer is it makes me remember how to talk. "Nostalgia," I say, and he laughs again.

Tina comes back out from the kitchen. "Benny says take your time, the pots and pans can wait." Then she busies herself behind the bar, sneaking glances at Graham. He's worth a glance or two. I don't remember him being so conventionally good-looking last night. Maybe the lighting is better here. His shoulders are disarmingly broad, and his eyes stupidly blue. Feet ever-so-slightly pigeon-toed in his combat boots. I forget how to talk again.

"So," he says, "nice weather, huh?"

Tina snorts and then covers it by clanking some glasses together. I seize on the subject of freak spring and tell him about the walk I went on before coming in to work. About Earl and the pawnshop guitars and my favorite river spot and this Vietnamese restaurant where you can get a sandwich for three bucks, which is where I should have gone when I got hungry, but I don't say that. I even tell him about the song I started working on last night.

"Will you play it for me sometime?"

I freeze. "I'll consider it."

Then there's a lull. He says, "So," and I say, "So," too. Tina laughs and turns it into a cough.

"So, are you busy Monday night?" he asks.

I feel like this is loaded. I don't know the right answer. "Umm, Monday...hmm. Today's Friday, right?" He nods. "No, I don't think I have plans Monday."

"There's this show happening on Albert. It should be pretty cool. My friends are playing. I recorded their album." He reaches into his jacket pocket and pulls out a cassette tape, which he slides toward me.

The band is called Good Sleep, and the cover is an illustration of a dog passed out, surrounded by beer bottles. "People still put music out on tapes?"

"Well," he says, "vinyl's too expensive to produce, and nobody wants to buy CDs anymore. But I can get you a CD if you don't have a tape player. Then you can put it on your computer or whatever."

"I have a tape player." I leave out the fact that I don't have a phone, since this seems to be going well and I don't want to test him with too many of my eccentricities.

"You do? Cool. Seems like a lot of people got rid of them."

"I'm a nostalgia major, remember?"

"Right." He smiles and then, remembering, searches his pockets again. "I brought you a flyer."

"Thanks."

"You're welcome." He gives me a rather formal nod, picks up his hat and puts it back on. As he turns toward the door, I'm already breaking the encounter down into parts I can analyze under a microscope in my mind until they make some kind of sense, but then he stops and says, "I haven't had the chance to work through the list you gave me yet, but I listened to a song by that Howlin' Wolf guy. You were right. He's amazing."

"My dog is named after him." I immediately wish for a hole I could crawl into, but he just smiles again.

"I forgot to say, I'm helping out at the show, so I can put your name on the list."

"Cool," I say, and he walks out. "Shit son," I say softly to myself.

Tina is shaking her head at me.

"What?"

"What do you mean *what*? What was that?"

"Nothing!"

"Ha!" She laughs. "Nothing. Yeah, right. That was young fucking love, is what it was."

"Uh, no. You're crazy."

"Hate to break it to you, Jo, but I know how to spot young love when it sits down at my bar in a leather jacket."

Benny comes out of the kitchen with a plate of food and puts it in front of me. Bless his heart. It's the deep-fried-every-thing special.

"Thought you might be peckish," he says, looking between me and Tina. "What's going on?"

I pull the plate toward me. "Hell's finally freezing over."

"Jo had a suitor in to see her. Young guy in a leather jacket with a lot of hair."

"Oh yeah?"

"Tina's having some kind of freak-spring psychotic break," I say.

"You shoulda seen it," she tells Benny. "She's got him wrapped around her finger."

"Not possible," I say.

"Why's that?" asks Benny, helping himself to a fry.

"Because I don't believe in love," I say through a mouthful of deep-fried potato.

They look at each other. "What do you mean you don't believe in it? Love isn't like a Sasquatch. Its existence isn't up for debate," he says.

I eat an onion ring and my taste buds rejoice. "I mean, I don't believe in it the way some people don't believe in abortion or organized religion or capitalism. I don't think it's any good for you, and I refuse to participate in it. I'd rather focus my energies on something that isn't guaranteed to one day fuck me up." I shove a fry into my mouth to emphasize my point.

"That's some big talk there, kid. You might eat those words one day," Tina says.

"Trust me, I won't."

"*Today's Friday, right?*" she says in a high-pitched, sing-song voice I'm assuming is supposed to imitate my own. I glare at her, and she laughs all the way across the room.

The rest of the night is low-key. Nothing out of the ordinary occurs—no more debates on the existence of love, no more drop-ins by confusingly handsome young men with unknown intentions. I tend to my dish pile, smoke some smokes. Benny has just told me to take off early when Winston shows up and slaps a pile of bills down on the counter next to me.

"What's that?"

"Your pay."

"Oh. Thanks." I put it in my pocket and take it out again when he goes. I'm getting paid again already? I count it once, twice, three times. On top of my hourly wage, I also get tipped out once a week too. I've already made enough to pay Maggie back and then some. I put the money away, then haul the mop bucket out the back door and dump it out in the alley.

Steam rises from where the water spreads, and I think about what I could do if I keep making money like this. I could really go somewhere.

∼

The house is empty when I get home, but a cloud of cigarette smoke hangs in the kitchen like a specter. Must have just missed her. I struggle for a few minutes trying to wrench the window open, but it's good and stuck, so I prop open the back door instead and let the freak-spring air flow in. Howl is lying on the floor, long dog legs all akimbo. I grab an apple and sit down next to her. It's been a while since we've had a good talk.

Hey, girl, I say. *How about this weather?*

Her rib cage rises and falls in a dramatic sigh.

What's wrong?

She looks at me, and I remember. Oh yeah. The letter. I'm still not ready to open it, so I get up off the floor, and that's when I find a note on the kitchen table. From Maggie. To me. Strange. We don't do notes. She says she's at the casino with Louie and that my school called and so did Ivy, and we need to talk. That last bit is underlined three times. I dial the number she's written beneath Ivy's name. "Tell me everything," she says when she picks up.

"Tell you everything about what?" I say, holding the phone away from my ear because she's yelling.

"Didn't Graham come see you today?"

"How'd you know that?"

"Because I'm omniscient. I know all, I see all. Even you, oh oblique one."

"Oh."

"No, dummy. He found me at school today and asked me where you work. How'd you think he found you? And why weren't you in Sinclair's class this afternoon? I took notes for you, but then I got paint on them. I think they're mostly still legible though."

He found her at school and asked about me. I want to ask why he would do a thing like that, but I don't want her to know how unheard of this is for me.

She laughs. "Stop playing coy. It's annoying. Gimme some dirt."

"No dirt. He just asked if I wanted to go to this show Monday night."

"Oh, he just asked if you wanted to go to the show Monday night. No big deal. Tuck, you're too much."

I shrug, but she can't see that.

"I was hoping that was it," she says. "I mean, I was going to invite you anyway, but this is better."

"Really? Well, I dunno if I'll go."

"Why not?"

"It's just…well, it's kind of weird, isn't it? I never thought I'd see him again after the way I acted last night."

"What do you mean? You were a hit!"

I groan. "Drunk and awkward is more like it."

"You weren't!" she assures me. "Really. Or maybe you were, but guys are into that."

"Don't humor me, please. I'm embarrassed enough already."

"No, seriously. You have this amazing broody thing going on. It's excellent."

"Broody?"

"Yeah, and it looks good on you, so shut up about it."

"I'm never leaving the house again."

"You're nuts. I'm telling you, you were totally charming. Graham liked you, and Graham doesn't like anyone."

"What does what mean?" It comes out a wail. Howl rolls her eyes. She's good at that, for a dog.

Ivy takes a deep breath. "It's not like he's an asshole. He's actually pretty nice, I think. He just seems really serious about the band, and maybe he isn't as social as Drew? Drew's always bringing people back to their place after shows, but Graham's a bit older and mostly keeps to himself. Comes off as kinda cold sometimes. Like you!"

"Oh."

"Don't worry," she says again, "I know you're not cold, just a bit…different. That's cool. I like different."

I'm worried she's getting tired of reassuring me, so I try to think of another subject to talk about, even though I want to ask her why and why and why again. Why does he like me? How can she be so sure? And what do I do with that?

"In any case," she says, "it doesn't matter. It doesn't have to be a love connection. Just come hang out with us. If you're not there, Drew and I will just talk about stuff that happened five years ago. It'll be no fun without you."

"Any night that is relying on me to make it fun is not one I'd place my bets on," I say, and she laughs, like she was waiting for me to say something like that, and I realize that's my role in this thing—to be charmingly self-depre-cating and a bit alien, but not too alien. And her role is to show me around planet Earth and teach me the customs of young humankind. It's a relief to know what's expected of me. We talk about other things, and by the time we hang up she's talked me into it. We agree to meet at the venue at nine on Monday.

⌒

I sleep in the basement. I do everything down here now.

SEVENTEEN

A strong spring wind blows grit into my eyes as I round the corner and head toward school. When the snow melts it leaves behind a layer of dirt, salt and sand, residue from a winter's worth of effort to keep cars on the road. City crews spend the first few weeks of spring scouring the streets at night with high-powered vacuum machines, but until they do and sometimes even after, it's hard to walk down the street without wincing. I narrow my eyes and put my head down as I approach.

Check me out, showing up on a Monday. Not even late. Early even.

It stayed warm through the weekend, and the snow is nearly gone now. What remains of it lingers in the shade at the edges of buildings, along the boulevards where the plows piled it high all winter and underneath cars that haven't been moved since freak spring sprung.

There's a frenzied feel to the temperate air. The smoking crowd at the western doors is three times thicker than normal, and as I come up behind the building I get caught between a couple of jocks tossing a football around with no regard to the flow of traffic. I step around Darren, the turbo-jerk in my English class, as his throw goes long, sending his buddy scrambling backward. Lesser students scatter, but one skinny niner guy isn't fast enough. The field became marsh-land over the weekend, and Jocko sends him sprawling into the muck. The kid scrambles to his feet, going, "It's all good, it's all good," not that Jocko thought to ask.

It's like the Wild West out here. A circle of tenth-grade toughs smoke a joint over by the bleachers, which are almost inaccessible because of Lake Football Field. A stoner guy teases a stoner girl, making like he's going to toss her in, and she laugh-screams like it's the best, funniest, most terrifying thing that's ever happened to her.

The hallways are worse. A crowd has formed around the school's token break-dancer, a white guy named Ryan whose parents let him put down one car's worth of linoleum in their three-car garage so he can practice his moves. He and the school's lone beatboxer bring a little suburban flavor to the school talent show every year. The rest of the time, their talents go unappreciated, except in mob-mentality moments like this. "Ry-an! Ry-an!" they chant as he executes a lopsided headspin. Administration is trying to break it up, which seems to consist of yelling, "Break it up!" at regular intervals.

It merges with the "Ry-an!" refrain to become something that sounds like an amateur remix of a club track.

English is half empty, and the half that did show didn't do the reading, myself included. Ms. Groves seems to have exhausted her reserves of giving a shit.

"Finish the reading and...uh...answer the questions on the handout." She waves vaguely at us from behind her desk.

"Ms. Groves?" asks a girl in the front row. "What handout?"

"Huh?" she says, staring out the window.

"What handout do you mean?"

"The one I handed out last class." The room is silent. "Did I not?" She blinks. We blink back. "I'll go copy that now, then."

The bell rings before she returns. I move to a seat at the front of the room and wait.

"Well, that was a bust," she says, dropping a stack of paper onto her desk. "They should just cancel class when the weather is like this. No one pays attention anyway."

I'm running drills in my head for tonight, trying to think through all the ways it could go.

"Jolene?"

"Huh?"

"I asked you how you're doing."

"Oh. I'm good. School good, family good. Good, good, good."

"You seem distracted."

"I guess a little."

"Want to talk about it?"

"Maybe. I dunno. Maybe not."

Thankfully, she seems amused. "Can I ask you a question?"

"Sure," I say, with obvious reluctance.

Groves gets up and starts digging through her desk. "Do you play poker?"

"Yeah. I mean, I haven't in a while, but—"

"Great!" she says, clearing the plants and some papers off her desk to set up the game.

~

Thirty minutes later I'm starting to reconsider Groves.

"I see you," she says, tossing a chip into the pot, "and raise you another fifty."

I glance at the small stack of chips in front of me. The surge of competitive feeling is foreign. When was the last time I played a game with anyone? Must've been before Matt left. I toss another chip into the pot. "I call."

We throw down our cards.

"Shit," I say.

Groves laughs a laugh that can only be described as a cackle and scrapes the pot toward her side of the desk.

"Do you always beat your students at cards?"

"Only when they let me."

"What if it's, like, hurting my self-esteem?"

"Do you have self-esteem issues, Jolene?"

I eye her warily. "No more than the next girl."

The cards are a comfortable blur in her hands as she shuffles. "It's not easy, being a girl these days."

I snort. She finishes dealing and turns on her electric kettle for the second time this hour. "You said it was your brother who taught you to play poker?"

"Yeah," I say, looking over my cards.

"You two were close?"

"Yep."

"What happened?"

"He moved to Victoria."

"That's pretty far away from here."

"About as far away as you can get without a passport."

"Had you two ever been apart before?"

I shake my head. I finally have a reasonable hand, and she decides to get deep. Figures.

"You must have been pretty mad at him."

I bet 100. Time to go for broke. "I guess I understand the impulse."

"What happened to him out there?" She sees my bet and raises another 100. That'll clean me out. I weigh the risks.

"He met some hippies, and they converted him to their bohemian lifestyle."

She smiles. "And what does that involve these days?"

"Smoking lots of weed and playing music on the street. Dumpster diving for food and bragging about it. That kinda thing."

I see her raise and call. We show our cards, and I groan.

"That's not fair. You were using diversionary tactics, brewing tea and probing my psyche."

"One more round? Or we can play a different game if you'd rather?"

I collect the cards and shuffle them with none of the deftness she displayed, then deal another round. I wonder what Graham meant when he said he wasn't planning on going to the Cal when I'm not around. I look over my cards. They're not bad in and of themselves, but they add up to next to nothing at all. Maybe it's time to bluff. I suppose I've got nothing to lose.

"Jolene?"

"Huh?" I flip another card over. Jack of diamonds. Doesn't help me much. Groves raises me another twenty, which is all I've got. I throw it in. "All right. I get it—you're winning."

"I asked you a question. Did you hear me?"

I shake my head no and flip the final card. *Fuck.*

"I asked why you think you're such a bad person."

"Huh?"

"Why do you think you're a bad person? Give me some evidence."

"I…what kind of question is that?" I glare at her, then at my cards. They're still shit.

"I don't know," she says. "A good one?"

"I don't think I'm a bad person."

"You're totally bluffing."

"Wasn't that the bell?"

"You can be a bit late. I'll write you a note."

"I have a test in bio."

"Okay. But I have some homework for you first."

"I know. I got it in class."

"No, special homework," she says, like I don't know.

"Lay it on me," I say, standing up and grabbing my backpack.

"I want you to write me a list."

"Like, a grocery list?"

"Stop playing dumb, Jolene. It's insulting. I want you to write a list that details all the reasons why you think you're a bad person. Show me the evidence. Because it's clear to me you do believe that, and I think it's worth unpacking."

I look at her in a way I usually reserve for my mother. She doesn't seem bothered.

"Alternately," she continues, really getting into it now, pleased with herself and her unconventional teaching methods, "you can say it right here, right now. *I, Jolene Tucker, am a good person.* If you can say it I'll scrap the assignment and you can go home and do whatever it is you do when you're not here. And might I remind you how often you aren't here. And how I've been smoothing that over with Vice-Principal Lambert and how I could stop smoothing at any point."

I open my mouth to tell her I'm as good as the next motherfucker, but she's right. I can't.

"All right then. You better get to bio," she says, holding her cards so I can see her hand. She had nothing. I could have taken her for all she was worth.

EIGHTEEN

I try to walk home, but the temperature is dropping, and it's back to freezing. I'm tired of battling it out against forces greater than I am, so I get on a bus and ride home with new resolve.

Groves says if one way isn't working, then it's wise to try a new approach. She says if you feel bad about the way things are, you don't just keep doing the same things, the same way, over and over again. She says what's important is that you get back up when you fall down.

I don't think Groves knows much about falling, but I'm willing to give being wise a go.

And so, a new approach.

That I will wear my best jeans to the show is a given. They're two years old and in their prime. I pull them on gingerly, taking care not to worsen the fraying below the back pockets. Soon they're going to reach a dangerous level of threadbare, and I might be forced to retire them, but for the moment they're the perfect medium blue, worn out in the knees and getting there everywhere else. I haven't washed them in months, break them out only on special occasions, but it's definitely a best-jeans night.

I take a swallow of the beer I snuck and consider the question of what to wear on the rest of my body. Maggie and Char have busted out the tequila and are deep into rehearsals downstairs. I don't bother tiptoeing down the hall to Maggie's room. The closet door is open, being too packed with shoes and clothes for it to shut. I sort through the rack, holding tops up to my chest and discarding them after a glance in the mirror. Every time I think I've found a plain black shirt, it turns out to have some slutty fatal flaw. I am forced to remember parent-teacher conferences in fifth grade, when Maggie showed up in a dress so tiny, some girl asked me if my mom was a stripper. I said, *No, she's a singer*. This was back when I still believed in fairy tales and other things my mother told me.

Finally I find what I'm looking for—a plain black tank top. I slip it over my head. It's loose on me, whereas she'd be over-flowing it, and just a little bit fancier than my usual. I shove the rejects back in the closet.

I need some kind of talisman, a good-luck charm. I go down to the basement and root through a box of Matt's clothes until I find an old plaid shirt. Then I stand in front of the full-length mirror in the corner and evaluate.

My shoulders are way too broad—they don't balance with the narrowness of my hips—my thighs are too thick by far, and my chest hasn't gotten the memo puberty sent yet.

My hair is the color they mean when they say mousy, and I'd be infinitely more attractive if my neck were an inch or two longer. But it'll have to do. Being able to take in all my physical flaws in a glance is probably my favorite part of being a teenage girl.

I hear Howl behind me, turn around and find her watching. She doesn't need to say anything for me to know what she's thinking. The letter. I step around her and climb the stairs, leaving it unspoken.

Maybe it's not a good idea to apply makeup in the basement light, but I sneak a few things from Maggie's stash in the kitchen and come back down to try. It's hard, putting on makeup without really seeing yourself. I put some stuff on my eyes and attempt to force my hair to do something other than what it normally does, which is nothing. Then I sit and wait for it to be time to go to the show. I feel like a bomb that might go off. I feel afraid of myself.

~

When it's time, Maggie comes into the hall and watches while I put on my boots.

"You look nice," she says when I straighten. "Where are you going?"

I shrug. "Out."

She looks me over, and I force myself not to squirm. "When will you be back?"

"I dunno. Never?"

"Come here," she says, going back into the kitchen.

I follow reluctantly. Char is smoking by the window, which she's opened a crack, engrossed in something happening on her phone.

"Sit down," Maggie orders, and I sit. She grabs an eyeliner pencil and takes my chin with her other hand. "Close your eyes."

I do. She touches the pencil in short little dashes along my upper lash line. "Open," she orders, and I obey. Her face is so close I can see the faint bleached hairs above her lip and the filmy coating of foundation on top of her real skin. "Look up." I look toward the ceiling, and the pencil traces along my lower lashes.

She puts down the pencil and steps back. Maggie is beautiful, if you're into divas who hang out in dives. She watches me for a very long time before swooping in and rubbing her fingers all over my scalp, her talons raking lines across my head as she messes up my hair. Adjusts a strand here and then there, hands me the eyeliner and says, "Take this. For touch-ups. A little grungy for my tastes, but you're gorgeous, my girl."

"Thanks."

She lights a cigarette. "You got something you want to tell me?"

"No," I say. "Do you?"

"No," she says after a while. "Good luck out there."

"Thanks."

In the hallway I check the mirror, ready to wipe off the eyeliner and fix my hair, but I actually look pretty all right. Go figure. On the front street I stop to put my headphones on. Patches of cloud are speeding by the moon. Char and Maggie are laughing inside. The thing about Maggie and me is that we could be strangers. We're not. But we could be.

NINETEEN

The place is one I've walked by, an old-man bar I guess the cool kids are repurposing. A handful of people stand by the doors, smoke from their cigarettes hanging around them like a personal fog. None of them are Ivy, though, and none of them are Graham either, so I go in.

The light inside has a red cast that makes everyone look slightly evil. I'm halted by a girl who stands guard at the entrance to the main room in a getup that's not unlike my own—plaid shirt layered over something smaller, hair deliberately disheveled—except she's extremely pretty in a pop-star way, the kind of pretty that completely controls your life until one day it fucks off, and then what? Maggie was that kind of pretty once. I've seen pictures.

The sign declaring *Cover* says it's five bucks, ten if you want a tape too. For a moment I worry door girl might be checking ID, but she just says "Hey" in a deeply disinterested manner and then searches the list for my name when I say I think I'm on it. "Jo or Jolene. I don't think he knows my last name."

She runs a finger down the page. My pulse mounts as she doesn't find me, doesn't find me, and I'm fumbling in my pockets for some cash when she says, "Jo Tucker?"

I nod. She gives me a blue stamp on the back of my hand. I touch it, and it smears into a bruise.

The bands haven't started, and I still don't see anyone, so I take a lap of the room. It's pretty packed, but I remember Ivy's approach and find a break in the crowd and then force my way through it, applying my elbows to the sides of strangers until they move. At first I expect retaliation, but they just look at me, go blank and turn back to their talk.

My pulse has been quickening with every moment that has passed without my finding someone, but now it slows. No one notices how alone I am.

I make it to the foot of the stage, and on it is Graham, working to untangle a knot from a cord. My hand rises to say hello, but then I drop it. I need a drink, need to find a mirror. Then I can be seen.

I ask the bartender for a beer and a shot, and my voice saying those words reminds me of Maggie's, which would be disturbing if I wasn't already kind of disturbed. Tina told me how to get served at bars while I'm still underage. Said it's all about what you order and how you order it. But people have always tended to assume I'm older because of my height, and the bartender barely glances at me. I lean against the bar and smile so I don't scare anyone, sip my shot, down my beer and wait to be drunk.

While I'm waiting, I look at the girls. I hold myself up against them to see if I'm doing it right. I see torn stockings and hot-iron curls, shirts falling off shoulders just so. I see a silver ring piercing the swell of a lip, and I see through a lace dress to the tattoos below. But I also see the effort that went into them. I see how close they got to the mirror to put their mascara on. How they stood back to assess themselves and decided they were hot shit or pretty all right or good enough before they let themselves leave the house, and maybe it's the whiskey, but I'm moved. I want to tell them they're beautiful and I appreciate the effort. It just makes me sad because I can't try. I did tonight, sort of, in my way, but my way's not right. I want to wear my clothes as Ivy does. As if she put them on a year ago and then forgot about them. As if she couldn't take them off if she tried. I don't even know what I look like. I'm not like Maggie and Char, with all their iridescence and adornments. And I'm not like the girls here, with their careful nonchalance. When I'm not in front of a reflective surface it's like I disappear. I can't recall what I look like. I mean, I can see a vague outline of my body, but no details. Nothing stands out in relief.

The band begins to play. Just the drums, beating, and then the bass, a rising, falling rhythm that relaxes somewhere in me—my spleen maybe. My hand takes the beer off the bar and my feet take me into the crowd, elbows aggressive now, hips turning side to side until I'm a few bodies back from the stage.

The crowd has a climate of its own. It's warmer in here by degrees, and you can feel the music on your skin, a sonic buzz. Against the bones of the song the guitars are a washed-out wall of sound, played by a girl and a guy, but she's at the center and plays and sings more. She sounds angry and underwater, and it's her I want to be. Not Ivy, not those other girls. The one onstage. I want to do what she does. I want to be the one who makes noise.

Pictures are being projected from somewhere behind me, dappling every face with color. No use looking for anyone anymore. I let the music loosen me.

A few songs later I still feel like magic, but I also feel like my bladder is uncomfortably full. En route to the bathroom I realize I'm drunk. My flesh feels different on my skull, as if it suddenly doesn't fit right. I'm sort of slack-jawed and hot-cheeked, like all the blood has gone there and left the rest of me empty. In short, I feel amazing.

The bathroom door won't open, so I throw my shoulder at it until it does. Girls stand at the sinks, pretending not to stare at themselves in the mirrors. I wait in a stall until I hear them leave, then wash my hands and take myself in.

I look weird and long and cavern-eyed. I look soft and dumb and over-styled. I run the tap, catch some water in my hands and rake my fingers through my hair until I feel better, until my effort from earlier is undone.

During the rest of the set I stand at the back of the bar and watch the soundman. He's sitting behind the soundboard with his back to me, and I think it's Graham but don't trust my eyes in this shifting light. So I just stand there behind him like a weirdo. I've never seen a soundboard up close. He adjusts a fader, and I try to hear what he hears, but before I can he turns and sees me.

I sit down in the chair he offers me through pantomime. The band has gotten loud now, and they play so hard they're glistening, and no one takes their eyes off of them except for me and Graham.

It's too loud to talk, but we try, taking turns putting our faces close and hollering. His lips are right next to my ear. I feel his breath, smell his beer, and I don't know what he's saying, but I know it's a question. I mime deafness, and we both shrug. It's too loud to try. So we sit next to each other and watch the band, and when I finish my beer he gets me another, and while he's getting it I reach over and turn up what I think is the reverb, to see how it sounds.

The first band finishes playing, and Graham goes to help the second band set up. Eventually I go get the next round, because he got the last. Then I wait behind the soundboard, trying not to stare at Graham, but it's hard when I have no one to talk to and nothing to do. Plus, I like the way his hair falls into his eyes when he bends over to plug in some gear, and how when he straightens up, he moves it out of the way to look across the room toward me. I think toward me.

He sits back down beside me when he's done. With only the house music playing, we can almost understand each other. "What happened to your hair?" he asks, touching it.

I tense. "What do you mean?"

"It's all wet."

"Right," I shout. "I took a bit of a sink bath before."

His laughter is delighted, and I am irritated/confused/flattered by this response. I wonder what other weird, true, unimportant thing I could say to make him laugh. I try a few.

⁓

The second band is assembling onstage when a hand clamps down on my shoulder—bony fingers that squeeze hard. Ivy is here. "You'll never guess what happened," she yells, but the rest gets drowned in music as the band starts, and she motions for me to follow her. I glance at Graham and then go after her. She gets us real close to the band and then stops and gazes up at the players. I realize she is one of those people who needs to touch everything, even, or especially, fire.

This band is the one Graham recorded. The lead singer is a sickly-looking guy, all angles, like he just had a growth spurt and hasn't filled out yet. But his voice is deep, and he sort of sing-speaks the lyrics with great authority. There's something anxious and neurotic about the guitars, and they grip me, reach into my chest and take my heart in their hands, squeezing the blood out. Ivy starts to dance, and then I do, mimicking her movements at first and then inventing my own as all around us motion spreads through the crowd, until no one is left standing still.

~

After the bands play, it gets a bit vague. People I don't know talk to me as if I do. I manage to perform cash transactions at the bar, and eventually we go outside to stand around and wait while the bands pack up their gear and get paid. My limbs are tired and good from dancing, and I know it's cold, but I can't feel it.

Graham comes out carrying an amp, and I grab the door for him.

"Thanks." He sets it down at the curb and reaches for his cigarettes.

"After-party?" Ivy hops around in front of me, possibly because she's only wearing her fur-lined jean jacket again and it's not at all weather appropriate.

"Good idea," Graham says. "Our place?"

Drew's eyebrows raise. "If you say so, boss."

Off we go, everyone, all together, the people from the bands and the tattooed girl and the one who worked the door. A whole pack of us headed to Drew and Graham's place over by the river.

When we get there, I stand around in the kitchen, wondering if I should take my boots off. No one else has, but they're tracking slush and sand in from the road. I'm surprised to find myself involved in a conversation with a girl wearing a giant tie-dyed T-shirt and a boy with a droopy puppy face. I have no idea what they're talking about, but I lean against the counter for greater nonchalance and nod along.

Through the kitchen door I can see Graham at the stereo, back to me, and I cross the room without too much trouble.

"Any requests?" he says.

"I dunno. Something funky but groovy?"

"Funky but groovy, huh?" He begins to search the records for something that might fit that description.

"Oh no, not actually. That's just an inside joke between me and...someone who isn't here. Sorry—it's stupid."

"No," he says. "I like inside jokes I'm outside of."

"Me too. I'd much rather infer things."

"Oh yeah, inferring's the best."

"Wow," I say, and then I say it again as I turn my attention away from him and to the records. The whole wall is stacked with milk crates filled with records, more records than I've ever seen. "Are these all yours?"

"This half is," he says, indicating the side we're standing in front of. The record player and its various components are on a table in the middle, and the crates continue on the other side. "Those are Drew's. We thought about merging our collections, but it would get complicated if we ever broke up."

"How are they organized?"

"Roughly by genre. But really rough. Pick something."

"All right," I say, surveying the extensive options for a place to start. "This is a lot of pressure. I wanna hear everything."

"Well then," he says, "Pick twenty. We've got all night."

I look at the floor and it looks pretty good, so I figure *fuck it* and sit down on the floor to get a better look at the albums. Also, it cuts down on my swaying. I see Ivy across the room, and we have a conversation using only our facial expressions. She gives me one that says, *You all right?* and I give her one back that says, *What could possibly be wrong?* and then we crack open and laugh.

Graham sits down beside me. "What's so funny?"

"Nothing."

"Good."

All night we've been doing this thing. This thing where we say one thing with our words but with our eyes we're saying another, and I don't know what it is, but it's significant.

"So was it a boyfriend?" he asks.

"Huh?" I'm running my finger along the spines to help keep track, pulling out albums that catch my eye.

"The *funky but groovy* thing. Was it an inside joke with an ex?"

He's the headlights, I am the deer. I can feel the panic on my face, and I try to rearrange it. "No," I say carefully. Not too fast—not so fast it's obvious I've never had an ex. "Me and my brother. It was this dumb thing I'd say whenever he asked what I wanted to listen to. We weren't actually into music that was funky or groovy, but my mom had this Australian boyfriend once, and he'd always say that…" I trail off. "He's the one that got me into music. My brother. He left me all his records and his guitars."

"Cool," he says. "I'd love to see them sometime."

"Um. Totally. Hey, what's this band like?" I point at random.

"The Beatles?"

"Right." I shrug. "I grew up in more of a Clash household."

He laughs. "That's awesome."

"Oh, don't actually put it on," I say, mortified because he's pulled out *The White Album* and is taking one of the records out of its sleeve. "What about this one?" I ask, grabbing an album I'd set aside and getting to my feet.

"Pavement? Good pick. Go for it."

He lifts the needle and the turntable stops turning, and he takes the old record off. I slip the new one out of its sleeve and put it on, and he lines the arm up with the grooves and I let it drop, and we do this together, without speaking, until the silence goes on so long that I burst out, "Thanks for letting me hijack the DJ position!"

"No problem," he says. "I like how you live for music."

I sense it's time to stop. I can feel the spins right around the corner, but suddenly it's like I've stumbled into a bad romantic comedy and I'm just drunkenly reciting lines. "No, not *for* it. I live *off* of music."

"Even better." He brushes my hair out of my face, where I like to keep it.

I put down my beer and ask him for water. While he's gone to get it, I talk to my cells. *Come on, cells. Metabolize the alcohol. You can do it. Try.*

Hey, look, there's Ivy on the couch. I swim across the room to her like she's a life raft, and she scoots over so I can sit. I try to think of something to say so that when Graham gets back we can all talk together and it's not just him and me and whatever that means. "Hey, so how did you start doing your graffiti thing? Is it graffiti—do you call it that?"

Graham returns with a glass of water and sits down next to me. I can act normal. I am. I just have to try.

We are less drunk now. We've reached peak drunk and are on the decline. People are leaving. I wonder if I should too, but then he says, "You can stay here if you want. On the couch. It's comfy."

I open my mouth but don't know what to say because I don't know what I want.

"Stay," he says. "I don't want you walking home this late."

So I say okay because it's easy, and we sit on the couch, the couch that I will sleep on. Drew goes to bed, and everyone else is gone. Graham puts a movie on, and I'm having trouble with my eyes. They won't stay open. They have to close.

TWENTY

I sleep until I can't not wake up. The room is bright, and I'm the only one. I start remembering things, then something stirs, and there is the boy. His eyes red, and bags under them. He steps in front of the window and darkens the light. Bends down and kisses me a kiss that's like a pillow to my face. Blots me out, erases me. I try not to let him taste my mouth even though it's open, because it's morning and I haven't brushed. He touches my face when he stops. Looks at me. "Let's get breakfast."

I drag body to bathroom. Cold water on face. No shower because of what it would do to my hair. Someone thinks I'm pretty, and I need to keep it that way. That means no water on the hair, and I can't wear my hat, or if I do I have to keep it on, commit to it. That's what I'll do. Put on my hat and let it hug my head. Then wipe off the makeup from underneath my eyes and put fresh lines along the lashes. Slap some color into my cheeks, and I look all right. I look as good as I'm gonna get.

We walk to the breakfast place without speaking, but it's so cold it feels natural, not talking, and then we're slipping into a booth and out of our jackets. There are menus on the table. I consider the shiny omelets, and the lamination makes me feel sick. The waitress comes, and I point at one and try to look alive. Now we'll talk, I think, but we don't. We don't talk when the coffee comes or as we peel the lids off the cream and tear open packets of sugar or when the eggs arrive and I shake the ketchup bottle until it loosens and floods my plate. When the bill comes I reach for it and he says no, and I let him pay with his debit card even though I have cash. "Thanks," I say as we put our layers back on.

"I like your hat," he says, and I think beneath his scarf he smiles.

⌒

I go straight from him to school. Why? I dunno. I dig suffering, I guess. Sure enough, Groves takes me aside after class and tells me Vice-Principal Lambert wants a meeting.

"Oh goody," I say.

"They called your house."

"Cool. I'll look into it."

"Did you do your homework?"

"Uhhh...jog my memory?"

"The list."

"Right." The list of reasons I'm an awful person. "No. I'll get it to you tomorrow. Shouldn't take long."

164

"I'm trying to help you, Jo."

"I know," I say, backing out of the room. That's the problem.

I stay on through lunch and bio and math. I even go to gym. I'm woozy, but we're just knocking volleyballs around, and I tend to be all right at that. The gym teachers always look at me with hungry eyes because of my height. But none of that can touch me. I hold last night to my chest, close, for comfort. I run through it in my mind and then I run through it again. The way I felt in the crowd, watching that band. The way the sound soothed me. Wandering from one place to another in a pack, like I belonged. Math class can't touch me, and bio can't touch me, and nothing can. I remember the way he leaned in, and then the kiss. I feel bigger and smaller than I've ever felt. I feel a hundred things I can't find words for. I feel totally unlike myself.

After school I don't want to go home. Everything I don't want to face lives there. But Howl's there too, and I'm tired and I smell bad and I should check to see if Benny's called about shifts. All the melted snow has turned to ice, and I drag my feet across the streets, skating home, hoping no one's there.

But I have no such luck. Maggie and Char and Louie are in the living room when I walk in. He's still here. That's got to be a record. I grab Howl and try to slip out again, but Maggie comes into the hall.

"Where were you last night, Jo?"

I don't answer. She tries to get between me and the door.

"I was worried," she says, and I stop. Not because she's moved me, but because I couldn't count the number of times she's gone out and not come home, and her playing the part of the concerned parent requires a full-body eye roll.

"Just come watch some TV with us. Louie made brownies," Char calls from the couch.

Maggie is still blocking the door. "You got a delivery today," she says in a different tone, as if she knows something that'll make me stay. "It's on your bed."

"I need to walk Howl. Do you mind?" I say, low so only she can hear.

"You better come straight home, Jolene Tucker," she says, but she doesn't sound convinced. She moves out of my way.

～

The river doesn't feel the same. I don't want to sit on the bank and look for proof that time is passing. Time feels different with Ivy and Graham and all of them. I just want to keep my head full of that.

Howl doesn't roam around the park. She stays close. Follows me around instead.

Where were you last night? she asks.

None of your business.

How original, she says. *But really, where were you?*

Out. At a friend's.

I didn't think you had any friends.

And I thought you were supposed to be my loyal companion.

You need to go home and talk to Maggie. About the thing that came in the mail today.

Fine, I snap. *Let's go home then.*

Before we get there I put my headphones on and blast my music. I don't look in the living room when we walk in. I drop my jacket in the hall and wrestle my boots off. I just don't look and I just don't listen, and I go down to the basement where the boxes are.

First I put his posters back on his walls. Then I put his clothes back in his drawers. And his shoes back on his floor in his corner by his mirror, which I am good at avoiding. I take the letter out from underneath the mattress and hold it for a few seconds. Then I put it back and lie down on the bed, close my eyes and hum his tune. Not one he wrote, though I remember those. One I wrote for him. They're all for him. Not about him. Nothing I write is ever about only one thing. Always three or four or five things. But they are for him.

I fall into sleep. Who knows for how long? Char wakes me, knocking on the door. Knocking and knocking some more. And saying and saying my name. I climb the stairs and sit down at the top.

"Jo?" she says, different this time, so I know she's heard me settle there.

"No."

"No what?"

"Just no."

"Okay, well, I'm leaving a plate of food out for you. You should eat something. You looked pretty haggard when you came in. You should take a shower, honey—you'd feel better. And you should talk about it too. Whatever it is. Whoever he is."

I stand up to go back down the stairs.

"Jo? There's something else. You got a delivery today. Louie signed for it. It's a guitar."

I go downstairs and play. I play the song I want to play for Graham, because it says everything better than I could. I play it loud, so they'll hear upstairs and know I'm not listening.

A while later I stop playing because my stomach hurts, it's so empty. I open the door slowly, carefully, but they've gone out. The plate isn't on the floor anymore, but it is in the kitchen. I take a bite and examine the house for signs. You can tell a lot by reading the traces they leave behind, if you know where to look. Maggie's signs are easy. Of course, the crowd of empties by the sink and the cloud of smoke are hers. The butts of Char's du Mauriers mingle with Maggie's Export "A"s in the ashtray, telltale lipstick marks on each, cotton-candy pink for Maggie and frosted beige for Char. Louie's signs are subtler. I read him in the well-stocked fridge and the organized shoe heap in the hall. I listen to the messages on the answering machine, hear the ones from school and erase them, though it's probably too late, then climb the stairs and look in my bedroom door.

There, on the bed, is a guitar case. It's covered in UPS stickers that declare it fragile.

I stop reading signs. I'm down the hall, I'm closing the bathroom door, I'm losing my clothes, I'm turning the shower on and stepping under it.

I do feel better after the shower and with some food. But then it's night, and I can't sleep because I already did. So I go back to the basement and play. I play the old ones and a new one that came from the things I've been hearing with Graham. I play them over and over and out.

TWENTY-ONE

In the morning there's a fight. Maggie gets the door open somehow and comes down, and it's bad. She sees the unpacking and says what have you done? And Louie comes down and stops halfway and stares, and I'm still a bit asleep and angry. To him I say what are you doing here, what are you looking at, who are you even? And to her I say you horrible mother. I say, it was your fault. I say, everything is always your fault.

And she says he's gone, you know. And I say how? Do you know? And she says, it's true, he really is. Gone. And I say you don't know that, there's no body. And she says Jo. She looks at me like she's afraid. Of me. And the tears stream down. And she says, they found it. Him. You know that. And her hand goes out for Louie, and he finds it. Where did that guitar come from, Jo? And I say get out. In the worst voice I can find. Get out of here you're the one who's dead to me you're the one who's never been there. I can't wait to get away from you. From here. And Louie says hey now, everyone needs to calm down now before you say things you don't mean. But we already did, or did we? Nothing makes sense. I was just sleeping and then this. She breaks away from Louie and throws herself up the stairs, crying so hard, and he looks at me for a minute like he wants to say something, but I turn away and hang my head so my hair falls and I can't see him and he can't see me, and I stay that way until I hear him go.

Like I said. Bad.

TWENTY-TWO

I wait until they leave, and then I go to school. Not mine. The other one. Yeah.

I go there and I sit at my spot by the escalators, where I haven't sat in so long. Or it seems so long. I think about going to the bus station and seeing what a ticket out of here would cost today. I think about the wad of cash in my wallet and the other one underneath my bed. I think about the letter that is also there. I think about how I can't go home and I also can't not go home. Because at the very least there are things to pack that I'll need. If I go. I'll need clothes and the wad and a guitar or two and maybe the letter because I don't know what it says yet. So I have to go home. Either way. Eventually. Mostly I just hear the things we said in my head in a loop. Then a voice says, "Hey!" in this really happy way, and I look up and it's Graham. And I'm foggy but happy too.

"I was going to call you last night, but I realized I don't have your number." He sits down beside me.

"Oh yeah," I say, and remember to smile.

He pulls out his phone and hands it to me. "I was going to ask Ivy for it, but this is better, because now you won't think I'm a dorky stalker for asking your friend for your number."

I don't know how to work his phone—it's fancier than any I've ever used. I mess up and somehow enter my name as *Jotuck* before I hold it out to him. "I can't make it work. Umm. My hands are too cold from being outside."

He takes it from me and then touches my fingers to his face. "No they're not," he says, but not like he thinks I'm crazy. Like he thinks I'm cute.

"Well then, your phone is just too newfangled for me."

He smiles. We both do. He puts my number into his phone himself, and I feel the way he makes me feel again. Good and new. "Well, *Jotuck*, I have to get to class, but what are you doing later?"

"I'm doing nothing later."

"Want to do nothing at the space with me and Drew? I'll ask Ivy too."

"Sounds good."

"How's eight?"

"Eight's good."

It's odd, the way he's looking at me. It's the same way he looked at me yesterday. Like he had to drag his eyes away. "I've gotta get to class," he says again.

"Me too."

"Okay."

"Okay."

"See you later then," he says. "At eight."

We say bye back and forth twice, and then I stand up, because I'm afraid if this goes on too long, I could get used to it. I gather my notebook, jacket and bag and wave as I head down a hall, any hall. I find a classroom with students filing into it and settle in for a lecture about economics, which I do not hear at all.

⁓

The walk down Portage toward Main feels uphill, but there are no hills here. Still. I feel it, like I'm being pulled backward, like my legs might give out. It occurs to me that I haven't eaten.

Earl sits at the counter where Earl always sits. He looks at me like, *Not today, kid*, and I look at him like, *Do you see me asking? I'm not asking for shit.* I go to the back, and I look over each guitar. I look each one in the face before I pick.

I play all my songs, one after the other and then over again. It's getting so I can't play songs by other people. I can only play songs by myself. When I stop, Earl is watching. He looks surprised. The clock behind him says I've played too long— it's time to go see Graham. "You're getting better," Earl says as I leave.

"Thanks," I say. And I feel good because it's so hard to tell.

⁓

We meet at the space, and he hands me a pill. Well, first he says hey how's it going, and I say pretty all right, how's it going with you, and he says not bad, not bad, and then he hands me a pill. "We took 'em half an hour ago. Quick. Catch up."

I put it on my tongue, because where else can I put it, and I swallow, because what else can I do? I don't even need water. It just washes down. I didn't know I could do that. But I'm trying a new approach. One where I swallow everything.

"Come on," he says. "Let's go up and find the others." He takes my hand as we walk to the elevator, and I don't know how to hold it because no one has ever taken it before. He lets go to unlock the door, and I feel better. But there are no others. And I feel worse.

"They must've gone up to the roof," he says, handing me a beer. I drink it fast, like medicine. Better. Then his hand's on my back. Worse. He gives me a milk crate to sit on, and we're talking about music, and he says play me your favorite song and passes me his computer, and it's better, it's easy, it's like before.

He takes the computer back and says listen to this song and then that one and I do and some of them I hate and the pressure in my chest of trying not to say it is tremendous, but in this state I know better than to say it because I'm better in this state. And then there are the ones that knock me back, tear at my heart, make me want to hate them like before. What is this? I ask him over and over even though it obviously pleases him when I want to know. I scribble the names he says on the pages of my notebook, or as close as I can get to them. He says you amaze me. He says you're not like other girls. And I write that down too.

Then the air begins to thrum, and the music is in the room with us in a new way—it's more with us than I've ever heard before. I see a flurry of letters I'm telling my hand to write. I feel a swell of something different in my belly, some new tide, and the edges of objects waver in their stride. Thoughts come to me easily and then melt away, and he sits across from me and the space in between us is shifting in size. But it's okay, because I know why.

From far away I can see it happening. We go up to the roof and wander around, and I don't feel scared of anything anymore. I don't remember why I was. He says look at the sky, and I do. It's a low, gray ceiling, and his eyes are hot shades of blue.

Ivy sneaks up behind me, grabs my head in her hands and yells, "WHAT'S GOING ON IN THERE?" in a tragicomic way. We laugh and laugh, but I don't think at the same thing.

"What time is it?" Drew asks like the answer will be outrageous, but then nobody knows, and no one reaches for their phone.

Finally Ivy looks and laughs. "It's not even bedtime for people who aren't on drugs."

I am saying something. I was trying to make a point, and then there wasn't one. No matter. We are perfect. We are all alive, and I never want to go inside. There's no sky in there.

The walk from the space to his apartment happens like one moment sliding to the next. I sit on the floor and consider the green tape on the ceiling that no one tore down when the paint dried, and the drip in the corner where one wall ends in another, and nothing looked like this before. I can see all my imperfections. All the flaws I am. The glass of water beside his bed. The lines of it. I don't need anything. Not one thing. I don't even need objects to still be there when I turn away from them. I take note of everything in equal measure. The rubber band around my wrist, the redness of my thumb where winter rubbed it raw and the circle of skin, moon blue, beneath the nail. Nothing looked this way before.

⁓

I go motor-mouthed, telling him things. Like how when I'm drunk I can sing, but when I'm not drunk I only sing silently. He asks me where I learned to play, and I say from my brother and from myself, and I tell him the story of the blues guitar and how all the strings snapped when we tried to bring it home. I tell him about the sound they made and how I like to chase it when I play sometimes, that sound. Then he says where's your brother now? And I say, oh, he's dead. He died.

"I'm sorry." He says it so fast. Rushes to meet it.

Nonono. My heart comes in like a drum. I say this song is great. I love the guitar sound. And I say do you ever feel too tall for landscapes like these? You know, because it's so flat. In every sense. It's almost obscene. And I say could you show me how to mix sometime? And I say I wonder where Ivy went and how long have you lived in this apartment and do you mind if I ask what the rent is and I put distance, distance between us and the thing.

He hands me his guitar and says, "Play." I take a deepish breath and do. I play the only song I can stand. The problem is that sometimes I want everything in front of me—I want everything around me. When I stop he doesn't say anything. Doesn't say anything for so long that I cover my face with my hands. He stands, so I do too, and then he's kissing me, and it's not the right answer, but I can't say yes and I can't say no, and it feels good from far away, and the rest doesn't feel good, doesn't feel bad, doesn't feel anything. It's just a thing that happened. It was bound to happen sometime.

TWENTY-THREE

His arm is on me, and his breath screams in my ear, and I don't like the way skin feels on skin. We're too close by far. I am still, and I count. The thing I can't stand is being heard. And seen. And felt. That's the thing. I get to ten, and I can't be in this bed, but it's so heavy on my chest, the arm. I don't know how to extricate myself from it, and I'm caught in these sheets, but I slip out a few inches, go slow and then fast, and I'm free. I can't find my clothes—I'm not wearing any. At the foot of the bed is a pile, so I grab it and go through the door. I find my jacket and find my bag and don't find my sweater and don't find one sock, and I stuff one foot into boot and then the other, and I leave, the way I've been practicing. The muscle must be getting stronger now. My head, on the other hand, feels a way it's never felt before. And also my heart. Other parts of me also.

TWENTY-FOUR

I go home and find a glass to fill with water and empty it three or four times, and then I go to the basement, lie down and try to sleep until it's time to work. You can't tell morning from afternoon from night down here. That's one of the best things about this place.

⌒

But I can't find sleep, or it can't find me. So I find a pen instead and write Groves her list of all the reasons I'm a bad person.

I don't always recycle recyclable materials. I take bus fare from Jim without asking first and I don't go to school when I say I will. I never answer the door when activists or Jehovah's Witnesses or kids selling chocolate come knocking. In fact, I've dropped onto my hands and knees to keep them from seeing me in the window on more than one occasion. Sometimes I see something that needs to be done and don't do it, like emptying the dish rack or saying,

Everything is going to be okay. When I walk by homeless people on the street I speed up and try not to look, and I have secrets. I don't floss and I tell the dentist I do and then act genuinely perplexed when he says I've got decay on the enamel between my teeth.

There must be something I'm missing. I could have sworn I was guilty of everything.

~

He calls in the afternoon. I pick it up when it goes to the machine, and his voice is in the room with me.

"This is a land line," he says.

"Yes."

"You live at home," he says.

"Yes."

He waits, and when I don't say anything he says, "Can I see you tomorrow?"

I say yes because everyone knows yes has always been easier than no.

"I don't want anything from you, Jo," he says before he hangs up.

But you've already cost me.

Only Howl can hear me now.

~

"You look like shit," Tina announces when I walk into the Cal.

"And also to you." I bow for some reason.

Benny is at the bar, drinking a coffee and making his produce order. "Sixteen lettuce, twelve cans tomato, two bags potato," he says, then repeats it like an incantation. When he hangs up, he too compares me to shit and then grills me. "What did you drink and when did you stop drinking it?"

I mutter something along the lines of *I don't know what you're talking about, there's nothing wrong with me, I'm just under the weather.*

"Just tell him, Jo."

"I do this for a living, kiddo. Hangover cures. I'm just trying to help."

"Winston wouldn't even care, not that we'd fucking tell him," says Tina. "So what did you drink?"

"Everything. I'm guilty of everything."

Benny starts to ask again, but Tina shakes her head, and he goes back to the kitchen to make me something.

The clamor of the slots is like nails on the chalkboard of my brain. Even my eyelashes are hungover. I don't understand anything.

"I should sign in," I say and don't move.

"Just let Benny fix you up."

I make a noise. An I-might-throw-up noise.

"Hey." Tina takes my chin in her hand. "You're going to be okay. You have to be. It's karaoke night. We need you."

But that's a lie. They don't need me. No one eats on karaoke night. They just drink and holler and hoot and throw up in the bathroom and in the corners and the halls. They just do tequila shots and fall down in the snow and call, *Encore!*

Encore! Until their voices crack and their hearts break and the streets close down with snow.

"Jo," Tina says. "You're going to have to pull it together a bit harder than that."

"Sorry." I didn't mean to speak out loud.

Benny comes back, and they look at each other in a significant way. I am so tired of people looking at each other in significant ways when I'm around. But then there is coffee. And a sandwich of fried eggs and cheese and eye of newt and tongue of frog and other mysterious ingredients I can't identify. It turns my stomach, and then it tastes good. It tastes like my feet are more firmly on the ground.

"How are we doing?" Benny asks, bouncing back and forth in front of me like a boxer. "We're gonna do this thing, am I right? That's right. Let's do this thing."

He slaps me on the back and it reminds me, but I'm too quick and push it away. I'm a boxer dodging blows. I can do this thing.

⁓

"Get out here. You need to see this."

"But do I?" I ask as I follow Tina out like a good dishwasher should.

A woman in hot pants and a halter top is slaughtering the karaoke competition. Tits out, everything out, she's using every inch of the stage. Winston's working the lights, but he can barely follow her. One minute she's galloping like a horse, and then she's twirling like a little girl. Then she's pointing and posturing like a pop star, popping hips and flipping hair. And then she is pounding the ground with her heels, stomping it like it did her wrong, and then she's kicking her legs up impressively high, given the four-inch heels she wears, the fuzzy pink ones she calls her inside shoes. She whips her boa in circles overhead, and feathers drift through the air. She's sweating, and her thighs jiggle, and her voice, singing along to the karaoke track, is pretty—there is a voice there—but she's working too hard, it's a sing-shout, a breathy rush to get the words out.

"She's changed it up this week. Not her usual fare," says a man at the bar who is tapping along with his beer.

No, it's not. As far as I know, she's always stuck to ballads of the where-is-my-man variety and anything that goes well with her impersonation of a sex kitten.

This is different. She is losing her shit. She is dancing like no one's watching. But everyone is. They are jumping and twirling and kicking along with her. The whole room is full of drunks cutting loose like a bunch of middle schoolers at the dance when their favorite song comes on.

"Something, huh?" Tina says.

The song ends, and for a moment she doesn't stop. For a moment she is still dancing and singing along to nothing. And then the silence hits her, and she halts. The crowd shouts their approval. They whoop rather than clap their hands, which are full of drink. Probably they can't tell that she is crying. Probably they think it's sweat running down her cheeks and streaking her mascara, but I can tell. Louie reaches up and helps her down from the stage. No one sings karaoke like my mother.

"Yeah," I say. "Something."

∼

At home in the basement, where there's no noon or night. I pick up my guitar—Matt's guitar—my guitar, and I play. When I play, I can't think. When I think, I can't play.

TWENTY-FIVE

I wake up before anyone. Early, actually, and not just for me. I get dressed in the basement and then go upstairs. Bodies everywhere. I recognize Cory and Char and George, the bouncer from the Cal, but there are also others I don't know. I heard them last night, up all hours celebrating. Maggie took the karaoke crown.

The soft *click-clack* of Howl's nails on the floor, and she's in the kitchen doorway watching me.

What?

She doesn't answer. She just watches.

It's not that big a deal, I say, and grab the leash to distract her.

But she barely follows me out the door, and at the river neither one of us is in the mood. She just sits and watches me, then wanders off along the path, but she doesn't sniff the trees or romp through the snow. And I don't try to measure the sun's progress across the sky or ask the river if it's melting.

When it's time to go I have to call and call before she'll come.

⁓

I wait outside the door to Groves's classroom until all the students have emptied out. She looks up from the papers she's straightening on her desk and then looks back down. "You can't be here, Jolene."

I was kind of hoping we could have lunch, and she could ask me where I want to go and then I'd tell her and she'd talk me out of it. But I can tell how it is—she's all business, arms crossed in the international symbol for *no bullshit*, trying to scare me straight. I shrug. "Whatever."

"I tried to help you," she says, "but there's not much I can do now. You'll have to throw yourself on Lambert's mercy."

"Wait, what?"

She blinks, reads the confusion on my face and looks resigned. "You didn't get the message? They've decided you've missed too many classes to pass this semester. You're on academic probation, meaning until you and a parent go in and talk to Lambert and the guidance counselor, you're suspended. They called your house to set it up."

"Oh." I'm surprised. Genuinely.

"*Oh*? Come on. Don't pretend to be too cool for school, Jo. I know you're not. You're upset. Admit it."

One more year of high school. In addition to the year I already had left. I told you time wasn't passing. I knew it.

"Jolene, hang on a second. I have to come in to school tomorrow to supervise the drama club's rehearsal. Mrs. Deacon is out sick. Come by at noon, and we'll make a plan. No one from the principal's office will be around on a weekend. Okay?"

I walk home into the wind. I tell my body to accept the cold, not to fight it, and I unclench, stop shivering. Tears stream backward out of my eyes, but they're not tears, really. Just water.

⁓

I stop inside the door and listen. Someone is home, but not Maggie, I don't think. Then again, I don't recognize her sounds the way I used to. They've shifted.

I grab the wad from underneath the mattress and throw it in my bag, hesitate over the letter, then leave it. What does it matter anymore, what the answer to my question is.

I stop and listen again. The first floor is still, but someone's upstairs in the shower. Quickly, quietly, I go up to my room to pack some clothes.

On the bed is the guitar case, *Contents Fragile* stickers plastered over it like *Do Not Cross* police tape. I unhook the metal clasps on the sides and flip the lid open. The whole time I was trying to find it, I worried I wouldn't recognize it if I did. Even the most familiar things fade fast when they're not in front of you. But I would know it anywhere. It even smells like him, like the lemon oil he used to clean the frets when he changed the strings. I reach out to touch them. Down the hall the shower turns off, and I focus.

I close the case, throw a change of clothes in my backpack and hurry downstairs. I'm stuffing my feet into my boots when I hear Cory call, "Jo? Where've you been? You missed a great party last night. Your mom was amazing! She won by a landslide. No contest. I was just using your shower. Mine's broken." He descends the stairs slowly, dressed but still toweling off his hair.

"Bye." I'm out the door, down the block, long gone.

⌒

Earl looks up when the bell on the door sounds, but when he sees it's me he goes back to his newspaper. I haul the guitar case up onto the counter and open it.

He looks at it for a moment, then at me. "What's this?"

"The guitar I was looking for."

He nods. "I can see why."

"How much will you give me for it?"

He leans back in his chair. "You spent all this time looking for it just so you could sell it?"

"Do you want it or not? I can go somewhere else."

He sighs, pushes his shirtsleeves up. "Kid, why don't you think this over? Talk to your mom about it."

I shut the lid, flip the clasps. "That's cool. I'll take it over to Sargent Pawn." I make to lift it off the counter.

"Hold yer horses. Bruce doesn't know shit about guitars. He'll rip you off for sure."

Earl sighs again, takes the blues guitar out of the case and looks it over in minute detail. I'm stunned when he starts to play, first a finger-picking country tune, then a swinging blues progression, then a rollicking rock 'n' roll number, then a pretty, lonesome melody.

"It plays well," he says. "I can sell it."

The price he quotes me isn't as much as it's worth, but it's enough. I sign where he tells me to and walk out with my arms swinging free.

～

Mullet lady at the station says there's an eleven o'clock bus to Vancouver and asks if I want a ticket. I stall.

"What about eastbound? When's that one leave?"

"Honey," she says eventually. "Come back when you know where you want to go."

～

I go looking for Jim.

The site where I found him the last time is over by the Forks, where two rivers become one. I walk there watching my feet, trying not to fall on the sidewalks of sheer ice. But the building has vanished, the lot smoothed over. There's a sign advertising the parking garage that's coming soon. In the meantime the empty lot gapes like a lost tooth. All gone.

The pattern that's emerging lately is simple. I do stupid things without realizing it, one thing after another. In that vein, I sit at a food court table and make the silent calculations of a lowlife. How long it will take me to pull myself together and journey over to the space if he does want to see me. How sketchy it would be to ask one of the guys who hang around outside the off-sales at the Woodbine to buy me a few king cans, and how much money I can afford to squander on a night that will probably prove to be just as pointless as all the other nights I've been leading lately.

I very nearly spring into action, but something holds me back. Could it be a last ounce of dignity? I thought I was all out of the stuff.

Outside the food court windows the sun goes down, but it's not night yet. I buy a coffee and watch the clock. Sometimes I remember to take a deep and necessary breath. Time passes on the sly. The clock doesn't move, and then it jumps ahead seven minutes all at once. I wait for it to be six o'clock. I sip my coffee and wait. When the hands of the clock are in agreement I cross the food court and use the pay phone to call Graham.

"Hello?"

"Hi. It's Jolene."

"Hey!"

"Hey." Oh, fuck. "So…tonight."

"Yeah," he says, "tonight."

"Umm, you said you wanted to hang out. Does that… offer still stand?"

He laughs, and instead of being relieved that he finds my awkwardness charming it pains me. But then, everything is paining me today. "Yes, it still stands. We were gonna go to this house party later. There's a few good bands playing. Wanna come?"

The security guard is circling me, checking his watch. I've gone over my thirty minutes. Also, making a call on a pay phone pretty much spells *drug deal* around here. I ask Graham when I should meet him, and although it isn't for another few hours and I've already gone everywhere I have to go, I say, "Cool, great, see you then," hang up and leave the food court before I get arrested.

In the mall bathroom I change my shirt and brush my teeth. A girl a bit older than me, in business-casual attire and a name tag I can't read, watches me, then pretends not to when I meet her eyes in the mirror. She must work in one of the clothing stores, or at least that's what I presume. And she presumes I'm one of the at-risk youths who hang out in the food court, selling drugs or buying them. We both wash our hands at length, as if to prove something, and then leave together.

Outside the wind blows and the buildings lean. My nose runs and my eyes do too, but my feet walk me slowly. I'm still a bit early. Got a bit more time to kill.

George isn't on duty yet, so I walk in the front entrance of the Cal and go down the hall to Winston's office without encountering anyone. Excellent. The door is open, and I can see him at his desk, bent over some paperwork. I knock.

"Jo, come in. I didn't think you were working tonight."

"I'm not. I have to tell you something."

Winston is a bit of an asshole, has terrible coffee breath, and whenever he talks about my mother it grosses me out—no matter how mundane what he's saying is, he manages to sound like he's leering. Still, this is hard. He's going to hate me. But I'm trying to liquidate my assets, and it only makes sense to collect the last of my pay before I decide what I'm going to do.

"Someone giving you trouble? Is it that beer delivery guy? I noticed him lurking around last week when you were working. I can get George to have a word if you want."

"No, it's not that. It's just...I can't work here anymore. It's...just not working out with school and everything."

Right away his eyes shift, so that now, instead of looking at me, he's looking through me. I've witnessed this before. He's pure capitalist, only sees what will benefit him in some way. Everything else gets shoved aside, bulldozed over. He sighs, exasperated. "I suppose you're here for your pay? Of course you are."

He gets up, grumbling, and checks the schedule, which is posted on the wall. Then he punches some numbers into a calculator, pulls out his wallet and counts off a few bills. "There you go, kid. I told your mom this wasn't a good idea, but she begged me to take you on. Said you were all messed up still from your brother's accident. You make sure you tell Benny on your way out. He put time into training you."

I leave without saying anything to anyone.

TWENTY-SIX

He comes down to let me in, looking too good, as always. Boys have it so easy. They don't have to worry about all the things I worry about as Graham and I say our heys and wait for the elevator. Things like how flat is my hair going to be underneath my hat, and is there anything hanging out of my nose that I should know about, and what if he wants what happened the other night to happen again? And what if he doesn't want it to happen again? He puts his hand on the elevator door when it opens, so that if I fall on the threshold I won't get crushed. Such a gentleman.

"Thanks." I look at the floor. And then him. And then the floor.

I didn't think it would be this much with us. What we did the other night. I thought it would fall away, forgotten, but I can feel it there. Between us. The silence strips me naked, more naked than I remember being before.

We start and stop talking at the same time.

"How's—"

"We should—"

I feel myself blush what I assume is a similar color to the one he's burning with. He starts again.

"We should talk later? Yeah?"

The doors slide open, and I step out into the hallway. "Yeah. Sure."

He smiles, and I am totally disarmed, disoriented. I cannot deal with the way this nice boy looks at me. What does he want to talk about? And whatever it is, what will I say in return? My head's so full of it, I walk past the door to the space, and he laughingly takes me by the shoulders and steers me back in the right direction.

"I have a proposition for you," he says. "I'll tell you later though!" This last bit he yells, because inside the space, Ivy and Drew have pumped up the tunes and are dancing like their lives depend on it.

"Hey!" Ivy bounces over to hug me, which is awkward because she doesn't stop dancing while she does it. And then I'm dancing too—I have no other option but to join in. At first I can't find the beat, but then I take off my jacket, then one sweater, then another, and I find it. Graham brings me a beer, and I stop to take a gulp. I'm always either too cold or too warm. Either sweating or shivering.

When the song ends, Ivy falls to the floor dramatically. Drew turns the music down.

"How do you feel?" she asks as he sits next to her.

He pauses in serious contemplation, then shatters it with a smile. "You're right, I do feel better. The dance cure worked." To me, he says, "I had the Tuesday blues. Ivy said she could cure me, but I didn't believe her."

"That was his first mistake," Ivy says.

"Isn't it Friday?" I ask.

They laugh. I've said one of those dumb-naïve things. Alien from the planet Uncool. "It's a drug thing," Ivy says. "You take some molly on Saturday night, and by Tuesday your serotonin levels have bottomed out."

Oh right, I think. The pill.

"We took it on a Wednesday, of course," she continues, "but the theory still holds. How're you feeling, Jo?"

Everyone turns to watch me ask myself if I have the Tuesday blues or not. I don't know if I do, but I'm sure that a description of how I am, were I able to articulate it, would send all of them running for the hills. Good thing we don't have any. "Just tired, I guess. I worked late last night."

"What's it like working at the Cal?" Drew asks. "When Ivy told me you worked there I didn't believe her."

"Why not?"

"Well…" He looks around the room for something— words, I guess. "I don't know. I guess you just seem too soft to be hanging around there."

I let my eyes go dark. "I'm not soft," I say in my best menacing tone, and they laugh again, because, despite what any of them might know about me, despite the neighborhood

I come from and the bar I work at and the torn jeans and the combat boots, I know my timidity is louder than all that, and it's what they see.

Graham reaches into the beer fridge and pulls out four more bottles in one giant hand. We retrieve them from between his fingers, and he sits down beside me on the little couch, which curls around us under his weight. "If anyone ever gives you any trouble, let me know, okay? I can meet you after work and walk you home."

This feels like the greatest kindness I can ever remember being given. This boy who hands me beers and says he wants to protect me. And yet, as he puts his arm around my shoulders and talks on to Ivy and Drew, I feel myself shy away from him. Fear rises in my chest and threatens the place I've found, and I shoo it into the back of my mind. I find an empty room and put it there.

"What about you? I ask Graham. "Do you have the Tuesday blues?"

"No," he says. "Quite the opposite."

Wincing at his mushy tone, Ivy gets to her feet. "I'm going to the roof for a smoke."

"You can smoke in here, you know," says Drew, who has recently dropped a butt in an empty bottle, swirling the last drops of beer around to put it out.

"I know. I just want to see how cold it is."

"Cold!" we all say at the same time. Then, all together again, we raise our bottles and drink to celebrate this consensus.

"Okay, okay," she says, pulling a can of spray paint out of her bag and backing toward the door. "I also wanted to do some painting."

"Cool," says Graham. "See you soon."

Drew grabs his jacket and goes after her. "I better make sure she doesn't fall." But he wags his eyebrows at us like he knows we want to be alone.

It's not that simple though. What we want. I get up and go back to the fridge, to get away from him, to get another beer. I drained most of my drink with our toast. "Sorry," I say. "I'm drinking all your beer. I should have brought some."

"That's okay. I bought some whiskey too. For when we go out later, to keep warm."

I see the bottle on the floor next to the beer fridge. "May I?"

"Be my guest," he says, eyes on his computer, where he's choosing another song. I take a swig that burns down my throat and turns my stomach when it gets there. But then I go warm and take another. Now that we're alone again I can feel it there. The fear I put away. It's at the back of my mind, burning brighter. Now that we're alone again I feel it between us, what we did the other night, what it meant, how much it mattered. I don't think I want it to matter much, but I don't know. In any case, the whiskey makes it matter less, and the music fills up the pit of my stomach. I sit back down beside him.

"I've been thinking about the other night," he says, and my body goes rigid. "I think I should record an EP of your songs."

Oh.

"No pressure," he says. "You don't have to play shows or promote it or anything. I just want to capture the way you sound right now."

"Oh," I say.

"I have all the gear we'd need right here. I could play drums on some of the tracks if you want, or keys or more guitar even—but only if you want, of course. They're your songs. And obviously I'd do it for free, and if you hated the result you could just delete the files and never show anyone. What do you think?"

I don't think. That's not what I do.

"You think it's a stupid idea. You hate it. Don't you?"

I shake my head. I don't want to lose this feeling by speaking, by making plans for a future that may not come, so I do the easy thing and kiss him.

TWENTY-SEVEN

When the others come back, we break apart, straightening clothes and cushions and hair, me quickly, him less so.

"So are we going to this party or not?" asks Ivy.

None of us know. We break the decision down.

Ivy checks her phone. "Katie will be there. And Kyle and Trevor and those guys."

"The first band is probably playing now, but we can make the second and the third if we go."

"Where's the party?" I ask.

"St. Boniface," Graham says. "It's probably, what? A half-hour walk?"

"Fifteen if we take the shortcut," Ivy says. Her phone buzzes. "Katie says the first band, whatever they're called, was great, and that everyone says we should get our asses over there."

"Let's do it," says Drew.

So off we go to the party.

Except we're drunk now, and we go slow. The whiskey makes the rounds of the room as we pack beer into backpacks and pull on hats and check pockets for smokes and the joint Drew's rolled for later. Graham switches off all his machines and locks the room, and we go down and out into the night.

At first I fall into step beside Ivy. "How are you?" she asks.

"I'm good." The whiskey almost makes me believe it.

"What happened the other night? I shouldn't have gotten so high—I sort of lost track of you. How did you get home?"

"Umm. I didn't?"

"Girl, we should talk."

She gives me a loaded look, because Graham's caught up with us now. He stays glued to my side in a way that could be construed as an effort to stay warm—it's not unheard of for total strangers to huddle together at bus stops and the like in the worst months of winter. But that's not it at all, is it? He talks to me more about how he'd like to record me, something about running my vocals through a particular guitar amp, and I listen peripherally while also tuning into Ivy and Drew's conversation, because really what he's saying may as well be a fairy tale. I could never really play for him. That one time was just that—a one off. But the sentiment, the fact that he heard me and what he heard made him want to record my songs, capture my sound, that keeps me warm as we take the street that skirts the river, heading toward the Forks.

At some point the road veers away from the river to make room for the train yard. That's the path we take, cutting across the field, following the tracks. Graham doesn't talk now, and the ground—grass covered in ice covered in snow—is unwieldy enough that I need to hold on to his arm to stay upright. He slips his hand into mine and squeezes it, and my hand surprises me by squeezing back.

Ivy circles an abandoned boxcar, pulls a can of paint from her backpack and traces a quick bird on its side. "Now you," she says, handing me her paint. "Draw something."

"I can't draw."

"Then write something. You can do that."

And I guess I can. I shake the can like I've seen her shake it and the write the first thing I think. It's harder than it looks. The wind carries a lot of the color away. And it takes a while to get the hang of how to make letters. I step back when I'm done.

"What does it say?" Graham asks.

"*Wish you were here*," Ivy reads. "Right?"

"Where's here?" asks Drew at the same time Graham says, "Who's you?"

"Shh," Ivy says. "Jo doesn't have to explain her art to you."

With that she starts walking down toward the river where the train bridge looms darkly.

I forgot about the bridge. The party is on the other side of the river. We'll have to cross.

"Hey, guys," I say. "Isn't the footbridge over there?"

"Yeah, but the party's just on the other side of the train bridge," Ivy says. "It'll save us fifteen minutes if we cross here."

The footbridge is better. The footbridge is not so bad. It's wide and smooth, and it's not hard to imagine its paved expanse is any old city street.

"You cool with that?" Ivy asks, falling back beside me.

"Yeah, 'course."

"It's super safe. There's plenty of space to walk next to the tracks if a train comes. I've done it before."

I stumble, but Graham is still holding on to my hand, and he steadies me. "Thanks."

"No problem." He smiles and suddenly leans in to kiss me again, and this time I don't like it. With Ivy and Drew right there, and the look on Graham's face like he knows me. I turn my face away and let go of his hand, but I'm not sure he notices because we're at the base of the bridge now. He pulls out the whiskey and it goes around again, and I feel better. Better than better. I feel brave. I guess that's what they mean by "liquid courage." I say thanks again and wipe away the courage that's trickling down my jaw.

"All right," Ivy says. "I'll go first. It's a single-file affair." She steps out onto the first wooden plank that runs horizontally across the bridge. Drew follows her. Graham stands back to make way for me, holds out a hand like, *ladies first*.

"No, you go," I say. A bit mean. A bit like I want to see the back of him. He blinks, and in his eyes I see I've confused him, and I feel relieved, because that makes both of us.

But then he turns and leaves me, and I hate him for that too.

I start to follow and then stop. Graham gets smaller, doesn't notice I'm not with him. He calls forward to the others, and they shout something back. I feel myself fracture, break away from their dark shapes. There are no lights around, only the full moon above, but it's bright enough to cast shadows, long ones that beckon and reach across the snow. I have to move now or they'll be way ahead and know something is wrong. Ivy's done this before. I can do it too. Think of all the tests I've passed lately, all the things I've done I thought I couldn't do.

The trick, of course, is don't look down.

That's the wrong thought to be thinking as I place my foot on the first plank, because I have to. Look. My heart thuds in four-four time, and I hold on to the railing and take another step. Graham's back is a flutter in the dark. Between the planks the quality of the darkness shifts as the ground falls away, and I move one foot and then the other out over the river.

They're unevenly spaced, the planks, and far enough apart that I think I could fall through if I slipped. It's not out of the question. This is the time of year people drown. You'd think the river would be thick with ice, but it's not. It was warm last week, and now it's moving down there. I can't see it, but I know it's there. The water. Flickering and winking up at me. And all around me are different kinds of dark. I force my eyes back to the bridge, to the planks I'm walking on. I move one foot, then the other.

The rumbling starts low, so at first I think I'm imagining it. But then the train emerges from the dark, and it's deafening. I flatten myself against the railing, but a bit too much—it's only waist high, and on the other side there's nothing. I steady myself as the train reaches me. Ivy was right—there is room to walk beside it. I force my eyes down now, make them focus on the planks so I don't get dizzy from the train surging by beside me.

I can't see them now, can't hear anything over the thundering train. I'm losing them. I'm not even close. I open my mouth to call out, but what could I say? Someone help me—I'm losing my shit? I can't hear anything but the train anyway, barrelling on and on, so close I could almost—

I stop. Close my eyes and stand still.

What am I doing with these people anyway? They know nothing about me, not one thing. Not even Graham, who looks at me like he does know. Like he likes what he sees. But he can't see. Has no idea what I've done, that I've broken the most important rule, the one where I always keep my feet on the ground. I'm supposed to keep my feet on the ground. Because we're not the type to get away with things. Around here anything can happen, and it very often does.

And then I know I need to take it back, need to undo what I've done. I try to race the train back, but the rumbling grows, fills my heart, head, lungs, as I jump from plank to plank without stopping now, without giving a thought to my footing, because I need to get some air, I haven't been able to breathe in way too long, weeks, months maybe, and I try to go a little longer without it, and then something goes wrong with gravity and I'm falling forward.

To my credit, I only scream after I hit the solid, snowy ground.

I crawl uphill away from the river until the earth levels out, and then I empty everything I've got into the cold, clean snow, and still the train streaks by. There must be something wrong because it won't stop.

And then it does. The caboose quits the bridge and the landscape opens up and I roll away from my vomit and look up at the stars. They laugh down.

I grab a handful of snow and scrub my face with it, scrub off the makeup that I never wear, scrub until my skin is numb. That's when I notice my palm, the one I held on to the railing with. It's completely blackened with soot and dirt from gripping the railing so hard. I rub snow into it too, but it won't come clean.

Someone is calling my name. More than one voice maybe. I look back at the bridge and see an outline that could be Ivy coming this way. I get to my feet and run. Because sometimes I operate on instinct. The kind that makes you put out your hand to break the fall.

TWENTY-EIGHT

I don't stop. Not when I get so winded my lungs seize up and I can't draw another breath. Not when the beers we packed for the party bang into my back with every step. Not when a rock weasels its way into my boot and starts cutting into the meat of my foot. Not even when the voices calling my name give out. I only stop when the tears come. Then I sit down on the curb, hug my knees and cry.

I can only think one thought at a time, and right now the thought is, I'm too sober, so I pull a beer out of my bag, crack it and suck down the foam. I sit there drinking and crying, crying and drinking, as the cold concrete freezes my ass through the thin fabric of my best jeans. I kill one beer and then another before my vision clears and my tears peter out. When I can breathe again I get up and walk north along the river, stumbling by playgrounds and warehouses and empty lots, dropping beer cans on the ground as I go, like a real live lowlife.

I've been drunk before but not like this. No, not like this, with the darkness I met on the bridge leaping and pawing at the limits of my vision as I walk, swatting it away and chugging down more beer to make it back off and leave me alone, but it won't. It wants me to remember. And I need not to. When I wake up in the morning I want my brain to be a clean, blank slate, like freshly fallen snow.

Thoughts pass through my mind and I look at them and then away. It's not snowing, but the wind is picking up what's already fallen and throwing it around for good measure. I let my feet walk me through the weather, all bundled up but still wide open to the cold. I deserved this. I was so stupid to think I could belong in their world. When I don't belong anywhere except basements and empty rooms. Pawnshops and bus stations. In-between places where you can go out in public and still be alone.

Why is it I can feel very high or very low, but I can't feel at all in between? I'm such an asshole that way. I think about Graham and how he'll never talk to me again, how I don't really care, because the way he looks at me sends doors slamming in my mind, and who knows what that means in the grand old scheme of things. Nothing probably. Not one damn thing. He liked the idea of me that I offered up, but he doesn't know anything about how I really am.

It's like every time I think I know the phase I'm in, something shifts and I can't tell up from down, left from right, right from wrong. I tried to toe the line, bide my time, showing up at school every day even though it clips my wings just walking in. I tried to hold everyone an arm's length or two away, but I failed and they slipped by. So I tried to be cool, to have friends, to let someone a little bit in, but things fell through the way they do, and I'm left with chipped shoulders and glory stories. It's the day in, day out aspect of life that feels like it might kill me. That's what it is.

I turn onto Main, and everything is familiar and oh-so-everyday. I trip over an imaginary crack in the concrete and catch myself. So here we are again. Walking home again. Feeling alone again. Asking the same old questions again and again. I laugh out loud at myself. It's pretty pathetic. I don't know what I want or who to ask for it, so I just walk and walk and think and think, and my head is full to bursting with all these thoughts, and there's nowhere to put them so they just float around, filling me up, taking up all my spaces. I reach out and touch the stucco of the building I'm passing, let my fingers run along the bumpy surface, scraping my skin, adding to the mess that is my blackened hand.

"Hey! Wanna ride?"

A car pulls up alongside me. A beat-up blue car with the windows rolled down. Two guys are inside, leaning out to leer at me. I look away.

Sometimes I realize I'm walking like my mother and I stop. This is not one of those times. Maggie has this "to hell and be damned" way of walking, leaning forward and charging ahead as if into battle. Not the girlie wiggle you'd expect.

I adopt her stance and speed up, but they've parked and jumped out and are after me now. All around me now. One at my side, pressing into my arm, and one in front of me, walking backward. They aren't guys. They're men, dressed too young in ballcaps and baggy clothes, wrinkles circling their eyes and stubble darkening their chins.

"Slow down," says the one in front. "We just want to talk to you."

The other one has my arm tight. I pull, but I can't get free.

"Let go of me."

"Chill, baby," says the talker. "We just saw you out walking in the cold, late at night, and thought maybe you wanted a ride."

I dig my heels into the ground and use my weight to wrench my arm free, but his fingers dig in deeper, and they back me up against the wall. His spray-can aftershave makes my stomach lurch. "I'm just walking home. My mom is expecting me." My mouth stumbles over the words, and even to my ears I sound afraid.

"Well then, be a good girl and let us drive you. Come on." He takes my arm, and when he does, the quiet one loosens his grip on me, and before either of them can tighten I explode out into the street, running straight across all four lanes, no thought to traffic. I hear them swearing behind me and hear the car doors slam, but then I'm down a side street, then a back lane, and I run for as long as I can and then keep going till I'm home.

I find my keys, put them in the door. Slam it shut behind me. All the lights are on, but no one's home. Howl is asleep on the kitchen floor, and I curl up next to her, bury my face in her fur. I would like the room to stop spinning, but it won't. Not even when I close my eyes or when I ask it nicely to please stop. Not even then.

TWENTY-NINE

Questions in the morning. Bad ones. Like, why does my mouth taste like puke, and what am I doing on the living-room couch, and why is Maggie sitting by the window in her bathrobe, watching me?

"You're up."

"What the fuck," I say, rubbing what feels like sand deeper into my eyes, "is going on?" And then I remember for the hundred thousandth time that I'm the original asshole. It's totally me.

The weight of remembering pins me down to the couch, but I need to get away from her, from everything, so I find a way to throw off the blanket that's covering me and sit up. Which on second thought is maybe not such a good idea. "Oh god."

"Here," she says. "Take these." She hands me Advil and a glass of water. "You'll be feeling pretty rough today."

I swallow the pills and catch a whiff of something that smells like hobo. It's me. "How did I get here?"

"You passed out on the kitchen floor. Louie carried you to the couch."

This is too humiliating to imagine, so I don't. The drapes are open, and delicate tendrils of light reach into the room, dance across the coffee table and the floor and stab deeply into each of my eyeballs. "What time is it?"

"A bit after two," she says. "I thought you needed to sleep it off."

"Shit," I say, standing up.

"Sit down, Jolene. We need to talk."

I climb the stairs in an entire catalog of pain, leaning forward and bracing myself with my hands like a Neanderthal or a toddler or maybe just a drunk. I'm beyond wounded pride at this point, but I'd still rather not face-plant in front of Maggie, and I'm none too steady on my feet right now.

Maggie follows me to my bedroom, so I grab a towel and leave again, shutting the bathroom door behind me.

In the mirror a strange girl with gray skin and matted hair stares out. I avert my eyes from hers and drop my clothes on the floor, turn the taps, let the water run until it's hot and step into the shower. Water scalds the skin at the top of my head and streams down my body, but I don't adjust the temperature. The pounding of my skull makes it hard to distinguish one pain from the other. So much the better.

The room is thick with steam when I'm done, but I'm still careful to avoid the mirror. I also avoid thinking about what

I'll say to Groves. I'm more than late. I may as well not even show. I push it away. I push everything away. Basically, I'm tiptoeing around in the corners of my mind.

In keeping with this avoidance theme, rather than go into my room again I start putting on the clothes I wore last night, but it's no use—they'll have to be burned.

Even in the state I'm in, I know it'd qualify as a warning sign to show up to see my English teacher covered in my own puke. Wrapping myself in the towel, I scoop up my dirty clothes and hurry down the hall to get it over with.

Maggie is sitting on my bed, next to the guitar case. "How're you feeling?"

"Fine." Bristling with annoyance or something masquerading as it, I pull open my dresser drawer and put on underwear and then a pair of jeans. If you've ever wondered if it's possible to put on underwear angrily, well, it sure is.

"Ivy's been calling for you all day. Last night too. Late. She was really worried. Something about a bridge."

I keep my back to her as I find a T-shirt and put it on too.

"Your school called too."

"Uh-huh."

"And Benny."

"Good for him."

"You want to tell me what happened?"

"Nope."

"What about the guitar? You wanna tell me about that?"

My hair is wet and in my face, and I am very, very close to crying, but the one thing I want right now more than anything in the goddamn universe is not to start crying in front of Maggie, so I brush my hair angrily, straighten my shirt angrily and walk out of the room.

"Where are you going, Jo?" She sounds so tired, it stops me in the hall. But it's too late. I've got to go.

⌒

Groves's car is still in the parking lot. I'm too chicken to go in and look for her, so I wait around outside, not feeling the cold. After about half an hour a group of students comes out. I can tell they're drama students by the way their voices project across the parking lot. Groves walks out after them, fumbling for her keys and pulling her scarf up over her mouth. I have to call out a few times before she hears. When she does, her face is hard.

"This is bad, Jolene."

"I know," I say, and then I start crying. I start crying like I've been saving up all my tears for years, and maybe I have.

"Hey," she says. "Shit, come here." She unlocks her car and shoves me inside. It's flood season on my face. And I don't care. I've moved to a place beyond pride. For a few moments Groves just watches me soak through the tissues she retrieves from her purse. But then some of the drama kids pass by and stare, and she waves, starts the car and pulls out of the parking lot.

"Are you kidnapping me?"

"Not yet. We'll see where the evening takes us."

"Where are we going then?"

"I'm getting you out of here. Or do you want to be a spectacle?"

This prompts another surge of tears. "But I already am!"

She glances away from the road to me. "So? You gonna talk?"

I press my palms over my eyes and try to stem the flow, but it doesn't work that way. I don't know where they're coming from. I hiccup, and it hurts. "I made an ass of myself all over town."

"How's that?"

I can hear the hint of a smile in her voice. I uncover my eyes. We're pulling into the driveway of a house a few blocks away from school.

"Come on," she says.

"Do you live here?"

"Sort of." She unbuckles her seat belt and opens the door.

"That's ambiguous."

"Good word," she says, leaning into the backseat to gather her bags. "You should have used it in that paper that was due last week."

"Why are we here?"

"Because," she says, "I'm going to make you some fucking tea."

Language like this from a teacher, even one like her, shocks me into calm. I get out and follow her inside.

The house is very seventies suburban. Busy textiles, orangey walls and fake wood paneling. In the kitchen she puts the kettle on, and I take a seat at the island.

"You really live here?"

"Well, I did. Growing up. I moved home last year to take care of my mom. She had a stroke."

"That's nice."

"Not really."

"Where is she?" I ask, looking around.

"Out. She goes to bingo with her girlfriends most afternoons."

"Sounds like my mom."

Groves takes mugs out of the cupboard, drops tea bags into them and gets the milk from the fridge. "I'm giving you Earl Grey," she says. "It's my feeling you need a bit of caffeine. You look like shit."

"I've been hearing that a lot lately."

"With honey," she says, taking it out of the cupboard. "Sweet things are soothing."

The kettle boils, and she pours steaming water into each mug, then sets one in front of me. "So," she says. "Talk."

And then we wait.

Eventually I shake my head. "I thought I could do it, but I can't."

"You *can* do it. You just have to try."

"No, you don't get it. I thought I could have things other people have. But I can't."

"What kind of things?"

"I dunno." I shrug. "Friends? Fun? A future?"

"What happened?"

I shake my head.

"Talk, Jolene. I can't help otherwise."

She's wrong. It's not easy. It's not the kind of thing you say out loud. But for once I'm more afraid of what will happen if I don't talk about it, so I try. "We were going to this party. We were walking there. I thought it would be okay, that we'd take the footbridge, but they wanted to walk across the train bridge to save time because they were cold—these people don't dress for the weather—and I didn't want to, but I did anyway because I didn't want them to know."

"Know what?"

"That I was scared."

She scoffs. "There's nothing wrong with being scared, especially of doing something stupid like that."

"It's not like that. It's not the kind of fear normal people have. I have reasons to be afraid."

"Why?"

This is the closest I've ever come to it, and I stop and wait for alarms to start wailing, for the walls and the ceiling to cave in, for the floor to open up and swallow me down, but I'm still here. So is the ceiling, and so are the walls. Nothing's moved. The words barely made a ripple in the room. So I try another and another.

THIRTY

I used to be hungry all the time, ravenous, single-mindedly starving. I swam once before school and then again after, and I was never very good at packing food to take with me—neither was Maggie—so by the time I got home at night I'd be insane with hunger.

That's why I didn't notice anything strange when the carpool dropped me off that day. I went straight for the fridge, took a swig of 2 percent and rooted around for leftovers.

Then someone called out from the living room. Said, "Jolene, can you come in here?" I didn't recognize the voice, but I went. Char and Cory were there. That was normal. But Jim sitting on the couch next to Maggie—that was not. Someone else told me to sit down, and from the way they spoke it was clear they'd planned it, but it was a shit plan because it wasn't possible to feel like anything that happened next was really happening. No one had ever said to me, *Sit down—we need to tell you something* before, and I hadn't even seen Maggie and Jim in the same room for years. It was like a TV show crossover episode where your favorite stoner dad and your favorite catastrophe mom join together in a story line so outrageously orchestrated it ruins both shows for you forever. Because when I was safely seated they told me there'd been an accident and Matt was dead, except that couldn't be, because Matt didn't do things like die. He would never do something like that. It was completely out of character. They should have delivered it in some different way, a way that would have made it possible for me to do anything other than sink away from them into myself. They should have told me in a way that made it real. They should have had Matt deliver the news himself. He would have done it better. He could do anything. Almost.

Here are some things that I know.

I know it was raining. (I checked the weather records for that night, among other things.) Not a hard rain; it was that fine, misty rain that doesn't fall but sort of surrounds you, the kind umbrellas are powerless against.

I know he'd climbed that bridge before, with the friends he made staying at the hostel, friends he told me about when he called from the pay phone by the harbor, the same harbor that the bridge crosses. He would have been able to see it while he slid quarters into the slot and dialed home. That would have been the view.

I know that the bridge, a huge steel structure, is capable of splitting in half and rising up into the air to let ships pass between its gates, and I know that when it's flat and at rest cars travel across it, joining downtown Victoria to the neighborhoods on the far side of the water.

I know the bridge is painted a blue that the skies don't get out there. I know this because Matt told me so during one of those few phone calls that came in the weeks he was gone but not for good. He said Victoria had plant life bursting from every nook and cranny. He said even the junkies and bums who slept on the grass by the harbor had a million-dollar view. And he said the skies out there were either clouded over or a phony Disneyland blue and that on clear nights the sky went a color he'd never seen anywhere but the coast— black saturated by a vibrant blue. He said it must be the ocean reflecting or something.

But this bridge, the Johnson Street Bridge, it's painted a prairie blue, the pure blue of an uncluttered sky. That seemed important to me when I saw it. I've looked at pictures of all the places he talked about on the Internet. It's another use of technology I'm not sure I approve of.

On the bridge there's a pedestrian path that's separated from the road by a metal partition. At a spot just a little ways out on this path the steel supports of the bridge conceal a ladder, and if you plant your bum on the partition and swing your legs over, you can access this ladder and climb up to a catwalk about twenty feet above the road. Walk along the slick metal surface of this catwalk to the center of the bridge, and you'll find another ladder. Climb it. At the top you pull yourself up onto a final catwalk, except this one is narrow, like a gangplank, with a metal railing on either side.

You are now high above the water and the road, and you hold on to the railing and walk out to the edge, where the catwalk ends. It's not quite the middle of the night but nearly, and lazy patches of fog drift down from the clouds to lap gently at the edges of buildings. You sit down and let your legs dangle. Maybe you brought a beer along with you, and you drink it and you feel good, magic maybe, like you left your hometown on a whim and went as far west as you could go before you hit the ocean, and you stopped there to rest a while and found something that was all new and only yours. And maybe you go away in your head to think about things. Things you've done and things you haven't done. Things you might do next. Maybe you just feel empty in a Zen sort of way. Or maybe you're feeling badass, and when the beer is done you let the can drop, and you listen for the splash and maybe there isn't one.

There are so many possibilities. I imagine them. It's a big pastime of mine.

But this next part is the part I don't know at all, can't piece together with common sense or research on the Internet. I can't track it down with a few phone calls, and I can't ask an expert. They don't have those.

The cops spoke to the people he knew out there, and to us, but in the end they could only call it an accident. But that's not what it was. That's too trivial a word for what it was. It was and remains a mystery. And it's so hard to accept a mystery. Show me someone who doesn't love answers. Give me one person. I'd love to meet them. Maybe they could teach me a thing or two.

So anyway, you're on this bridge. And you sit there and do whatever, and when you're done you stand up, out there on the catwalk, past where the railing ends, and maybe the height gets to you or your feet fail you, and you fall.

Falling is easy.

And what happens after the fall is beside the point.

It's something else that haunts me.

I know how long the moment after your feet leave the ground lasts. How it stretches out and breathes. That's what I hate to think. That's the awful thought that comes to me when I'm alone at night trying to sleep, when I'm walking down the street with my head full of music only I can hear, when I'm sitting in class playing blind, deaf and dumb. It comes upon me regularly, the thought. I don't want it to, and I really wish it wouldn't, but it comes. What it must have felt like in that moment after his feet left the bridge and moved out to somewhere else. How long it lasted. How much he must have wanted to go back.

I know how it feels to me, and it's the worst feeling I've ever felt. Wanting to go back. And I do. I want to go back and back and back again. Back before yesterday and the day before yesterday and the year before that. Back before traffic interrupted time. Before cavemen had clothes. Before we took liberties, tripped fancies and lived these lives of endless leisure. Back to before I knew what it was to beg of gods we were never brought up to believe in.

That's what I want. That's all.

THIRTY-ONE

I leave Groves's house and let my feet go. Past parking garages
and boarded-up buildings and discount retail stores. I walk
past the university and the library and the big old beauty of
the Hudson's Bay building with its windows full of featureless
mannequins in jaunty spring fashions. By the hockey arena,
where people dressed in coordinated colors are milling about
before the game. I walk by broken bottles and cigarette butts
and puddles of frozen vomit that may well be my own. I walk
by kids pushing grocery carts down the street to get their
kicks and by a woman wearing three jackets who tells me
that her face is melting and by a girl with a baby bundled into
a stroller, waiting for a bus to come by with room to let them
climb on board. I walk in circles and straight lines, and I walk
in triangles and hexagons.

I don't think about anything, but then the sun goes
down and stays down, and I get cold, though it takes a
while for me to notice in my condition. And it wakes me up.

Snaps my mind back. Reminds me of the letter. And I want to know what it says. I need to.

At home I go straight to the basement, before anyone or anything can stop me. At the bottom of the stairs I stop, and my hand goes to my heart in surprise.

"Hey, sweets," Maggie says. She's sitting on Matt's bed, blanket wrapped around her, and she smiles at me through her tears. She stands up, and I start to turn around, run away, but I'm so tired that suddenly I'm sinking, to the floor, to my knees, and she's right there. She helps me up and sits me down and tucks the blanket around me. "Jesus, Jo. Your lips are blue," she says, and I guess I wasn't done crying after all, because I start to blubber all over again. But Maggie doesn't seem to mind that I'm snotting all over her shirt. She just holds me, and I let her.

⌒

A while later the door opens at the top of the stairs, and someone hesitates, listening.

"Baby?" Maggie calls up. She insisted I let her give me a pedicure. Said that there's nothing like having pretty, pampered feet to make you feel better.

"I made cookies," Louie says. "Would you like some?"

She looks at me. I nod.

Louie comes down and, to his credit, doesn't look at all rattled by the state I'm in. I remember what Maggie said about how I passed out on the kitchen floor and he carried me into the living room. It's too embarrassing to contemplate, so I shove it aside again.

"Thank you," I say as he hands the plate to me. He stands over us for a moment and then pats me ever so briefly on the head before going back upstairs.

"Tilt your foot this way, babe," Maggie says, maneuvering my foot into an impossible position. Otherwise it actually feels kind of nice. She rubbed lotion into my feet and pushed my cuticles back and cut away the extra skin around my nails with these sharp little pincers. Now she's filing them down, rather violently.

"Have you been climbing mountains in your spare time or something? Your calluses are crazy."

"Kind of," I say, spewing cookie crumbs.

"So," says Maggie. "You gonna read that thing or am I?"

I take another bite. The cookie is still warm, chocolate chip, and I feel the life force in me grow stronger as I chew and swallow. The letter is on my lap. We've been sitting here staring at it for, oh, a couple of hours. Howl comes over and puts her face on the bed, asking permission to jump up. I pat the space at my feet. "No, I'll read it."

"Louie baby?" Maggie hollers. "Can you make me a hot toddy for my throat?"

The envelope is addressed to me, postmarked Alabama. I try to tear it open carefully, to preserve its integrity for all time, but whoever licked it, this Tim Berland, did a thorough job, so in the end I just rip it open, take the pages out and read.

THIRTY-TWO

Dear Jolene,

I owe you so many apologies. The first is for the fact it's taken me this long to get in touch with you. I left Victoria months ago and have been traveling ever since. When I finally landed at my new winter home in Alabama, your letter was waiting for me. I had my mail forwarded down here from Victoria, but I never imagined there would be something so pressing, or I would have made some other arrangement. I'm sorry to have left you hanging. I hope you didn't lose faith.

The second apology is for buying the guitar in the first place. I'd been keeping an eye on pawnshops around Victoria for months, with the idea that I'd get myself a new ax to take on the road after I retired. I'm old now, you see, and my retirement present to myself was a motor home. Never in a million years would my twenty-year-old self have thought I'd go that way, but here I am. I had this fantasy that I'd drive around in my RV, parking by the Mississippi River and playing music while the water flowed by.

Even old-timers can be romantic fools. When I saw your brother's guitar it actually took my breath away. I knew I couldn't walk out of that pawnshop and leave it there, where it so clearly didn't belong. But I should have known that someone would come looking for a guitar that beautiful.

In your letter you say you just want to know who has it, where it is. You offer to buy it back at whatever price, if I'm willing. I'm going to send it back to you, though, trusting that the good people at UPS will deliver it safely. I'll get it off to you in a week or so, to give the letter time to arrive. I think it would come as a shock for it to just show up on your doorstep, but I also don't want you to feel like you have to respond, because it belongs to you and you should have it.

Which brings me to my final apology, and I warn you it's a feeble one. I am so sorry about your brother. Matt. I'm so sorry about Matt.

My wife, Edith, died fifteen years ago this July. She was diagnosed with cervical cancer that spring, and by summer she was gone. It was so fast. That was what hurt the most. How fast it was. I can't imagine how you must have felt when Matt died. How many ways it must have hurt. So please, allow me to return the guitar to you. And if you'll lend an old dog an ear a little while longer, hear what I have to say next.

Edith's been gone for fifteen years now. Fifteen years down the line, and I don't think about it, but I think about it all the time. By which I mean I don't think about the sad stuff anymore. I think about how she was obsessed, actually obsessed, with keeping squirrels out of the garden, and how I hated it because she set up these humane traps and when she'd catch one she'd call me at work, too scared to go out in the yard, and make me come home and drive the culprit out to the park to set it loose, and I'd be damned if it wasn't the same exact squirrel digging up the garden again two days later. She said that was impossible, but I swore up and down it was true, that the beans and tomatoes she grew were so delicious, squirrels would walk for miles to get to them once they'd had a taste. I think about how beautiful she was first thing in the morning with creases from her pillow still on her cheek. I think about her laugh. How easy and often it came. I think about the ridiculous sayings she picked up from her farmer father, which came out at the oddest times, like when we visited the Grand Canyon together a couple of years before she died and she stood at the edge and looked out for a good long while and then said, "Makes you feel like a fart in a hurricane, doesn't it?"

What I don't think about is how or why she went. It's the other stuff that stays with you. I hope having the guitar back brings you some peace, Jolene. If you hang in there long enough, I know you'll find it.

All my best,

Tim Berland

THIRTY-THREE

I look up from the pages. Maggie is bent over my toes, which are painted a hot, glittering pink. "Pretty gorgeous. Am I right?"

"I think I did something really stupid."

She sits up straight and gives me this withering side-eye. "What?"

I tell her and she stands up, sending all her nail supplies scattering. "Jesus, Jo, I thought you were pregnant or something, but this is way worse."

She whirls around and crosses the basement, shaking her head. "Louie! We're going out! Go warm up the car!"

"Maggie, wait. Where are you going?"

But she's up the stairs already. I pull out the dumb foam things she shoved between my toes and follow. Howl and Louie are in the front hall, looking confused, and Maggie is putting on her coat, a fake-fur one that makes her look like she's dressed up as a sexy cavewoman for Halloween.

I grab my jacket and am about to put my bare feet into my boots when Maggie shouts, "Stop!"

"What?"

"You'll ruin the polish! Here." She digs around in the shoe pile and finds a grimy pair of flip-flops. "Put these on."

"Seriously?"

"I didn't just spend two hours squinting at your feet, probably giving myself a few new wrinkles, just so you could smear my handiwork all over the insides of your old-man boots."

"Okay, okay." I slip on the flip-flops and follow her out the door. Howl whines loudly to come along. She never does that.

"Bring her," says Maggie. "We might need backup."

"Come on then." Howl bounds out the door and jumps into the backseat. I climb in after her, brushing the snow off my bare feet. Louie is behind the wheel, and he cranks the heat for my sake. Maggie has trouble navigating the narrow space between the car and the snowbank in her high heels, but eventually she gets one leg in the car and then drops the rest of her body in. "All right," she says to Louie. "King's pawnshop. Over on Main. I'm gonna kill that bastard." She cranes her neck to look back at me. "You got the cash?"

I do. Louie pulls the car out, and it lumbers down the street, which is rocky with accumulated ice and snow, not to mention potholes. I move closer to the warmth of Howl.

Don't worry, she says.

"Why not?" I ask. When I have so many reasons to.

"What was that?" Maggie says over her shoulder.

"Nothing."

⌒

Maggie unbuckles her seat belt before the car has come to a full stop. The shop is dark behind all the junk in the front window.

"He's closed, Maggie. Let's come back tomorrow."

"Not a chance." She gets out of the car and sticks her head back in to look me in the eye. "Give me the money."

I reach into my pocket, pull out my wad and count off what Earl gave me for the guitar.

"Jesus, that's all you got for it? What a fucking criminal. Stay here—I don't want you catching cold. Louie?"

He gets out of the car and leaves it running so I don't freeze or perhaps in case we need to make a quick getaway.

"Earl!" Maggie shouts, pounding her fist against the door. "Earl! Get out here right now! I know you run a card game in the back on Saturdays. Earl!"

Louie stands by, and I realize for the first time how he'd be sort of intimidating if you didn't know him. One of those barrel-chested men, sturdy as a piece of furniture. A good guy to have around if you need to shake down a pawnbroker for a guitar.

Deep inside the shop a light goes on, and Maggie gets louder. "I swear to God, Earl, you think I'm gonna get tired and go home? Not fucking likely. You messed with my kid, old man. Get your ass out here. Earl! Eaaarrrrl!"

The man himself appears, makes a show of looking through the glass to see who's knocking, as if she hasn't made herself abundantly known. He turns various locks and opens the door a few inches. I can't hear what he says—no one is as loud as Maggie—but he's shaking his head, looking over at me inside the car. I raise a hand to say, *Sorry I sold you my brother's guitar and then changed my mind; it's just that I was too sad to do anything else.* It's a lot to convey in one hand gesture. I'm not sure it comes across, because Maggie's yelling again.

"Go on! Go inside and get it then."

Earl disappears into the shop and Maggie turns to Louie, who steps closer and puts his hand to her cheek. It's a motion that stops me, takes me out of the moment, out of my hangover, which is raging on, and makes me realize something I think I've been trying not to realize. Maggie is in love. Actually. With someone who loves her back.

I'm still absorbing this when Earl returns and hands Maggie a slip of paper. She takes it and gets back in the car. Without the guitar.

"What happened?" I ask as Louie circles around to the other side of the car.

"So the thing to remember is, it's gonna be okay. We're not going home until we find it, okay, hon?"

I sink into the seat. "What did he do with it?"

"He sold it."

"Already?" Howl crawls farther onto my lap.

"Apparently when something good comes into the shop, he has certain buyers he takes it to direct. Louie, baby, do you wanna bring Cory with us, or do you think we'll manage on our own?"

"We'll be fine," Louie says, smiling at my mother. "You're much more intimidating than Cory."

This is true, but no comfort to me.

The address Earl gave us is in River Heights. Louie pulls back out onto Main and drives us to the fancy side of town.

⁓

"I'm coming," I say, unbuckling as we slow to a halt in front of a two-story house on a dark, unpopulated street. It's a nice house but by no means palatial, though the snow blanketing the roof and the evergreen bushes in the front yard do make it look pretty fucking picturesque.

"Don't be ridiculous," she says. "You can't go out in flip-flops in this weather."

Right, I'm the ridiculous one. But I resist the urge to fight. This matters too much. "Do you at least have a plan?" I ask as she checks her lipstick in the side-view mirror.

"The plan is to be persuasive," she says. "Gimme the rest of your cash."

I hand her what remains of my dishwashing wad.

"Jesus, Jo. You've been holding out on me." She gives me an appraising look, more impressed than pissed off. "We'll talk about this later. Let's go, Louie."

The first floor is dark, but upstairs the lights are still on. I see her press the doorbell, and a few seconds later press it again. Lights go on downstairs, curtains rustle in the windows that flank either side of the entrance, and then a man in a bathrobe answers the door. He's in his fifties, I'd say, but I can't make out much more than that from here. Seconds tick by. Louie stands to the side, appears to let Maggie do the talking. At least I think she's talking—her back is to me, and she seems to be using her hands for emphasis. The man had crossed his arms after answering, but they come uncrossed as he steps back and opens the door wide, and Maggie and Louie disappear inside.

Shit.

No, I think it's a good sign, Howl says. *Don't worry.*

But I am worried.

You're holding your breath again, Howl says, nudging my chin with her nose. *Don't do that.*

What if Louie is a violent criminal and he's putting the screws to this nice, normal man who just thought he was acquiring a quality instrument to keep in his living room and bust out for occasional Woody Guthrie jams?

Louie isn't a violent criminal, Howl says, tilting her head at me.

How do you know? I wail.

Because I know Louie. He's a building inspector for the city, and he's a hell of a cook, and he's in Maggie's support group.

There's some movement inside the house, shapes passing in front of downstairs windows and then upstairs ones too.

Wait, what? What support group?

The group grief counselling Maggie goes to every Monday.

I didn't know that.

Yeah, ya did, Howl says. *It's one of the things you forgot on purpose.*

Oh. I frown, puzzled. My head's not working right. I think I might have killed some important brain cells last night. *Why is Louie in grief counselling?*

Howl's eyes catch the streetlight shining across from us. They're the brightest thing in the car by far. *His daughter passed away from cancer five years ago. She was nine. Then his marriage fell apart. He's been going to the group for years. That's how they met.*

How do you know all that?

Because, she says, *I pay attention to my family. It's my job.*

Before I can respond we're both distracted by action at the front door of the house. Louie emerges, turns around and shakes the hand of the man, who steps back to make way for Maggie. She walks out carrying a guitar case in one hand, waves and makes her way carefully down the path in her heels. I hear the trunk pop open, then slam shut.

"Well," she says, sliding into the car. "We got it back."

"You did?" I ask. My voice is desperate, pleading. Louie climbs in and starts the engine. "How?"

"Easy," she says, handing me my wad of cash. It's surprisingly thick still.

"You didn't do anything bad, did you? Did you have to threaten him?"

She laughs. So does Louie. "Not even," she says. "We had a friendly, grown-up conversation, and he agreed to be reasonable. Just asked that I give him what he paid Earl for it."

"Are you serious?" I thought for sure it would take all my money to buy it back, if we were lucky. "Really, tell me. What did you say to him?"

Louie steers the car down the street, and Maggie reaches over to take his hand. "I told him the guitar belonged to my son who died, and that my daughter sold it as part of her grieving process, but then regretted her decision and wanted it back."

"Oh."

"Sometimes the truth is more effective than a lie, kiddo. Or a threat."

"Should we go out to celebrate?" Louie asks.

"Should we?" Maggie asks over her shoulder.

"No. I just want to go home."

THIRTY-FOUR

I sleep deeply for what feels like days, but really it's only most of one. When I'm finally able to rouse myself, I find the guitar case leaned up against the desk in my upstairs room. Downstairs I can hear the TV, hear Maggie and Louie talking in the kitchen. He says something in a low voice, and she explodes in laughter.

I take the guitar out and sit back down on the bed. I don't play. I just hold it. The guitar blogs I've been reading to educate myself say that when you buy a new guitar it's important to break it in by playing it daily and in different styles. As sound moves through the guitar the wood absorbs it, is altered, so you have to play quiet and loud, hard and soft, pluck and strum. The vibrations course through the molecules of the wood and change it.

I'm too scared to play it yet, because it might sound like the things he went through, the places he'd been.

But it feels good being close to it. I climb back under the covers and place it down by my feet. Howl noses the door open and comes in. She climbs up on the bed too, careful not to disturb the guitar, and we stay that way, quiet, for a while.

~

Six months earlier I'd started looking into the question of the guitar. I knew that if he'd sold it before he left, he would have sold it to Earl, who denied and denied it. So I started looking farther afield.

They sent us his backpack and his clothes and his body turned to ash in a box, as if that was proof enough. But nobody mentioned finding a guitar. He would never have gone anywhere without it.

So I started calling around. I called the hostel and got names. Matt was the kind of person you remembered, even without what happened. He made friends everywhere he went, and I found them. I found Susan, who worked at the front desk, and through her I found Riley, who said he'd jammed with Matt and that they'd talked about starting a band and that he was sure they would have really gone somewhere, if they'd had more time. I talked to the suspiciously named Dragon, who told me that Victoria is a hotbed of paranormal activity and that Matt had really tapped into that, really felt it, and that must have been why he'd stayed, must've been why he went up there that night. Dragon wouldn't say he'd been up on the bridge with Matt, only that lots of people climbed it for kicks. It was something to do, and there was a great view. I could tell he'd been up there with Matt, though, because his voice took on a guilty pitch when he talked about how it was like a spiritual experience. That when you got up that high you felt far away from some things and closer to others. Someone must have shown him the way. At least told him that you could climb it. Matt and I did those sorts of things, but we never went that far.

I got nothing from the hippies, so I started calling pawn-shops. Maybe someone had stolen it from his room after he died and then sold it. There was a pawnshop a block away from the hostel, but the man there, Steve, who I imagined as a west coast Earl, denied seeing it. He denied and denied it, until I offered him a hundred bucks, at which point he located a receipt that said he'd bought the guitar for three hundred dollars from Matt Tucker. The handwriting was Matt's—I made Steve send me a photocopy. And then what? I asked. And then I'm not sure, said Steve, so I sent him more money, all I had left, what I'd been saving to pay off the phone bill before Maggie could find out, and he remembered. He remembered selling it to a guy by the name of Tim Berland. He sent me that receipt too. I insisted.

I'm not very good at the Internet, but Tim Berland wasn't hard to find. A quick search turned up one man by that name who'd recently retired from teaching in the anthropology department at the university. I emailed and I called and I wrote, but I got no answer. I impersonated a former student and found out from a secretary that he was traveling through the southern states before settling in Alabama for the winter. She gave me an address, and I wrote one last letter. And then Maggie found the phone bill, and I stopped. I found new ways to pass the time.

I don't know why Matt pawned the blues guitar. Three hundred bucks wouldn't get him far. It was enough to rent a room at the hostel for a month. It was also enough for a ticket home. I don't know what he wanted badly enough to let go of it, when it was the thing he worked so hard for. When it was the thing he loved.

~

On Monday Maggie goes to my school, and somehow—I do not want to know how—she gets them to agree to welcome me back after a week's suspension. There will be consequences, but in the meantime, I have the week off. Sure, she drops a stack of homework that's higher than Howl on my bed, but it's a small price to pay. For the first couple of days I claim to still be recovering from the terrible hangover I gave myself the night of the bridge, but beyond that I just enjoy the act of convalescence. I stay in bed and read and write and play guitar. I take nap after nap, and I eat everything Louie puts in front of me. I let Maggie field my calls, and I put up with Char getting drunk and forcibly cuddling me while Baby tries to chew a hole in my mattress. They all talk around what's wrong with me, but it's okay. I know we'll talk again, and I know they just want to be close to me because it makes them less afraid.

Midweek, Ivy invites herself over. Or maybe Maggie told her to come. I wouldn't put it past either of them. I hear them shouting at each other in the hall. Not that they're mad— they both just have loud speaking voices. I go to the stairs and listen for a minute, hear them talking at the same time, about swimming and school and Louie and how Ivy got her hair that color.

"Hey," I say from the stairs.

"Hey!"

"You're up!" Maggie shouts. She turns toward the kitchen, where I presume Louie is hiding. "Louie! Make something for Jo and her friend to eat, would ya?"

"Mom, don't order him around like that. We're fine."

"Actually," says Ivy, "I could eat."

Maggie's eyes are shining as she goes into the kitchen to oversee Louie's latest efforts at fattening us up. I don't know if it's that I slipped and called her mom or if it's because an actual physical friend has come over to see me or if she's just high from the thrill of bossing Louie around. Hard to say. In any case, I invite Ivy down to the basement, because it's more grown-up down there than my real room is. I've been avoiding her phone calls because, try as I might, I can't think of any way to explain why I ran away on the bridge without sounding totally insane.

But Ivy is distracted by the basement, exclaiming over the décor. She approves of the instruments. "I've got no idea what this does, but it looks impressive," she says of my loop pedal. And she then begins to apologize and won't stop.

I listen for a while and then tell her it's okay, but she won't stop saying sorry for the bridge, sorry for forgetting I'm not old enough to be in university, sorry, sorry, sorry.

"I thought you'd finished high school early or something since you're super smart and everything. I mean, when I saw you in class, I just assumed. But I shouldn't have assumed. Even though you clearly don't like answering questions. I should have pressed or figured it out on my own or something. And I should have protected you from Graham! I'll kill him! Do I need to kill him? Because I will kill him, totally."

"It's okay, Ivy! I forgive you, completely and entirely."

"Are you totally sure you don't want to punch me in the face? Come on—it'd make both of us feel better."

"I'm not going to punch you in the face."

She starts to say something, but the words get caught somewhere between her throat and her mouth. She takes a breath and starts over. Serious looks strange on her. "My older sister went to school with Matt, you know. She told me when she heard. I wanted to tell you how sorry I was, but there was just that one swim meet where, well, you know... and then you quit and I didn't know how to find you. Besides, we only sort of knew each other, and I didn't want to force myself on you. My mom is always telling me that I have no respect for boundaries. But that's no excuse. I should have reached out."

I wasn't expecting this, and it makes my eyes fill again. Groves told me the other day when I couldn't stop crying that I might be weepy for a few months because I had beat it back for so long. She says I have to let it pass through my system. She says it's okay if it takes a while.

Ivy reaches out and squeezes my hand, and I give her a watery smile and take another minute to compose myself. The thing is, nobody knew what to say to me. So they said nothing. And so did I.

"Sorry," I say. "Don't kill Graham. He's not a bad guy."

"Are you sure?"

"Yeah. It's just…I dunno. I'm not ready for that sort of thing. I just thought I might be for a while. He's okay though."

"Well," she says, suspicious, "if you insist."

"He's been calling. I suppose I'll have to deal with him eventually."

"Oh yeah? What's he have to say for himself?"

"I dunno. I haven't picked up yet. But he told our answering machine that he was sorry, that he should have remembered I was afraid of heights."

"You're not going to keep seeing him, are you?"

"I have no idea," I say, and I don't. Like Groves says, I just feel like I need to be very, very gentle with myself right now, and my instinct is that means no boys.

Ivy leaves not long after that, promising to return. I put on my layers and take Howl to the river, sit down on the bank to think about stuff. Like how Ivy said I quit swimming before she could find a way to reach out to me. Like how I have to stay here because I haven't done everything I need to do yet. Like how maybe that's what made Matt stay out west the way he did. Not because he didn't want to come home, but because he hadn't done everything he needed to do yet.

Sometimes when I was swimming I'd imagine all the water vanished, that very quickly it was all gone, and then there was just air, and I was falling through it. That's what it was like when he died. Like the bottom dropped out of my heart, and I fell through it.

I only competed in one meet after it happened. I'd already paid the entry fees and everything, so it seemed like I may as well. I remember standing on the block as the official called us to our marks. I crouched down, grabbed the edge of the starting block and balanced on the brink. Ivy was there next to me, in my peripheral vision. When the shot rang out bodies arched out over the water on either side of me, but I didn't move. I'd forgotten how.

The starting official came over and put a hand on my back, helped me get down and walked me back to my team. He could tell something was wrong, I guess. And something really was. I'd lost it. The ability to make the decision to let my feet leave the ground. I couldn't go there anymore, couldn't take the moment that comes before you fall. It didn't matter that the water was only three feet below. I couldn't even be that brave.

Coach was pretty nice about it. Gave me a Gatorade and told me we'd get them next time. But I could tell he was a bit disappointed that I hadn't been able to turn the sudden, world-halting loss of my brother into junior provincial swimming victory. The Monday after the meet I walked out

onto the pool deck barefoot in my street clothes and told him
I was quitting. He took it like a champ, got just a little teary
and told me I could have been great, that I had an Olympic
reach. He meant my arms, which are freakishly long, and
my hands, which are freakishly big, perfect for grabbing on
to the water and putting it behind me. That made me think
about how Matt had always told me I had great guitar hands.
He'd taught me a few basic chords, but I'd never been serious
about it. After I quit, though, when I didn't have swimming
and I didn't have Matt and I couldn't even use my voice to
sing the songs we'd played together, I started practicing,
teaching myself. Turns out there's more to playing guitar than
just having the hands for it, but I'm trying. And, like Groves
keeps telling me, it's okay if it takes a while.

THIRTY-FIVE

After my hangover convalescence ends, things go more or less back to normal. Except that normal is different now. I get mad at her sometimes. Maggie. So mad it paralyzes me, my blood pressure shoots up and I can't breathe or see or think about anything except that I'm so mad. Why did she get it together after he was gone? Why did she wait that long? Couldn't she have held down a job, found a decent boyfriend, remembered to take her pills, before he left? Why did she let him do everything for her, for me, for us?

But then the anger fades, and I can see the real-world Maggie, the one outside my head. She's trying. She's doing better than she ever has. And that would make Matt happy. So I have to let it be real.

Groves says I'm an overthinker. I had no idea that it was possible to overthink, but she says it is and that I do it, and I have to admit, I sort of trust her these days. It's just that I want to understand. It's important to me. And so much of it

I *have* come to understand, more or less. I get the need to run away from here. I feel it too—it's just more complicated for me. I'll never be able to do what he did, cut and run. How could I do that to them after everything? But I do get it. It's so fucking flat here, so far away from everything, that it starts to feel like there really isn't anything else. I guess what I'm beginning to understand is that you can kill yourself asking unanswerable questions. I know what I know. I'm through beating my head in with regret. He loved me and he left and when he did that didn't stop. I loved him and he died and when he did I didn't stop.

Sometimes I get afraid the way I used to. Afraid of the quiet and what I might hear in it. Afraid of losing things I have and not getting things I want. When that happens, I take Howl to the river and sit with the fear. I stay still with it.

THIRTY-SIX

The moment I let go of the last note of the song, Graham leans into the computer and starts moving things around. I pull my headphones off and he gives me a thumbs-up, staring at the screen.

"That one was good," he says.

"You think?" It comes out whiny, but I don't care. This is hard.

"Yeah, definitely." He sounds more sure of himself than I've ever sounded in my whole life. He hits keys and moves the cursor around the screen too fast for me to follow. My vocals are the purple squiggly line, I think, and my guitars are the green one. We've already got those. That was pretty easy. It's the vocal take I'm worried about. That has to be exactly right.

"Can I hear it?"

"Of course." He plays it from the beginning, and we sit still and listen to my song.

It took weeks for me to make the call, for me to ask him if he'd still be interested in recording me. I knew I needed to explain myself first, but I didn't know how to tell him what I felt, because I didn't know what that was. I do like him, but I can't—not now. It wouldn't be fair or wise or any of the ways I'm trying to be.

So in the end I just told him I'm sixteen, and that worked pretty well.

There was silence on the other end of the phone for a good couple of minutes after I got the words out.

"You're in high school," he breathed.

"Yes," I said.

"I—you're in twelfth grade? That's crazy."

"Well, eleventh. And they almost held me back, so…"

"I'm such a creep."

"You're not a creep."

"Yes, I'm a creepy, creepy creep."

"You're only twenty-three," I told him. "In boy years, you're actually younger than I am."

"Are you okay?" he asked. "Did I…damage you?"

In my head I laughed and told him not to flatter himself. Out loud I said, "No. Not at all."

When I told Maggie how he reacted, she said he was a good one, that I should hold on to him until I'm legal, but I'm learning to take her advice with a grain of salt, or four hundred. But I do try to take it. She knows a thing or two.

The song ends, and he starts fiddling with levels again. "Slow down," I say. "Tell me what you're doing."

"Sorry, I'm just excited. I've got all these ideas for your sound."

"Come on, it's *our* sound at this point."

He looks stricken. "Shit. I overstepped. I'm sorry. I can back off if you want—"

"No, I like collaborating with you. It's fun. I just want to know what you're doing there."

He smiles. "I like collaborating with you too. So, what I want to do is really soak the guitars."

"When you say soak?"

"I mean saturate them."

"And when you say saturate?"

"I mean like, drown them, or like—"

"I'm kidding. Saturate makes sense. Go on."

"And then I want to bring your vocals forward, make them gigantic. How do you feel about doing some backing tracks?"

"I feel okay about it. But no gross harmonies."

"Right, only non-gross harmonies. And see, here this sounds a bit honkier than I'd like, but I can take the honk out." He hits *play* and I listen hard for the difference.

"It's more…"

"Roomy?"

"Roomy. Yeah. I like space."

"Yeah, me too."

"We're spacey," I say, and he concurs.

He scrolls through a menu of effects.

"What are you doing now?"

"Tweaking the mix a little. Putting some effects on your voice."

"Don't do too much yet. I'm not sure I like that take."

"Seriously? You can do it over if you'd like, but I think that one was great."

"But I sounded so...I dunno. Imperfect."

"Great—that's what we're going for."

"Maybe that's what you're going for, but I'd like to sound polished."

"No you don't. You just need to get used to hearing yourself. We'll take a bit of a break and then listen again."

"Okay," I say, getting up to stretch. We've been trapped in the space all day. My eyes are bleary from squinting at the computer, and my throat is hoarse from singing. I feel kind of fantastic. "Hey! I thought of a band name."

"What's that?"

I pause a moment for suspense. "Proofs."

Even though I obsessively pondered band names for weeks, coming up with untold numbers of shit ones before I thought of this one, after I say it I'm instantly paranoid that it's stupid and he'll hate it. I pick up my guitar and start noodling around nervously.

"I like it," he says.

"Good. I like it too."

"That sounded cool," he says when I stop playing. He sits down behind his drums and watches my fingers. "Keep going."

I've been thinking lately. Not overthinking, I'm pretty sure, but thinking an appropriate amount about how I used to spend my days trying to kill time. And all the days in the week, and all the weeks in the month, and all the months in the year, they were always on my mind. But the thing is, here's the thing—sometimes we fall into holes. It happens to the best of us. The wonderful thing about time is that it's always passing.

ACKNOWLEDGMENTS

I'd like to thank Tim Wynne-Jones and Shelley Tanaka for feedback on early drafts. Sarah Harvey for her keen eye. Julie Sheehan, Susan Scarf Merrell, Lou Ann Walker and the rest of the faculty at Stony Brook Southampton. My MFA classmates for their support of my work and for general help surviving the Hamptons (Emily, Alison and John especially). Both sides of my big book-loving family, my grandma Noreen, my parents Becky and Ian; and my siblings Binesi and Sam. Thanks to Ann, Leah and Maryam Decter for harboring me at various times. All of my writing teachers, really, but especially my mom and grandpa. My friends Anna, Carly, Julie and Jen, for not forgetting me when I go away to think about things. Teresa for the letters and Nic for all of it, and everything.

NORA DECTER grew up in the North End of Winnipeg, Manitoba. She has an MFA in Creative Writing and Literature from Stony Brook University and a BA in English and Creative Writing from York University. Though she now lives most of the year in Toronto, Ontario, she wrote the first draft of *How Far We Go and How Fast* at a cabin in the woods in Manitoba. She has a rock 'n' roll past. For more information, and to hear the songs Jolene plays in the book, visit noradecter.com.